The Man That Everyone Forgets

Liam Adams

Cover illustration by Liam Adams

The Man That Everyone Forgets

by Liam Adams

everyoneneedsaliam.com.au

We think this book is mostly suited to children from 10 years old, and young adults, 12 and over, although older adults may enjoy it as much!

This book is sold on the understanding that it is the work of a person with intellectual disability and Autism. All creativity is from the author and the text has been edited by his mother to the best of her ability. However, it is understood that the writing may be different from that expected in a formally published novel.

Liam hopes you enjoy reading his book as much as he enjoyed writing it. He would love to hear your feedback; if you wish to contact him his email address is ltahm@icloud.com

Canberra, Australia

June, 2025
ISBN 978-0-6455970-7-3

Acknowledgement to Creative Australia

Liam was absolutely thrilled to receive a Grant from Australian Government through Creative Australia, its principal arts investment and advisory body, that allowed him to write, self publish and sell 2 new fiction books: The Cursed Planet and The Man that Everyone Forgets. The grant is part of Creative Australia's Arts and Disability Initiative. Thanks so much to the wonderful Creative Australia!

Table of Contents

Preface

It may not help much or change anything, but they were willing to help their friend, even if this might be for the very last time. So, they were willing to do it all together.

I came up with the idea of this novel when I was travelling in mid 2021. This had to be my thrive period, as this was the same time I also began brainstorming my stand-alone epic novel, *Shifting Dimensions*.

At this time, I wrote the first drafts of the first five novels of the Librarian Saga, so I knew there was more to come in the series, even a few others I did not write at that time.

I wasn't as clear on whether this was the sort of story I wanted to write for the series. Almost all the other books, I thought of during in 2019-2020. But while we were traveling, I started to write some ideas out for this novel.

A few ideas came randomly. The first parts I wrote as it flashed me back to when I was much younger when you go to these water parks or kids play areas. I used to imagine about these as if I was on some strange world or if I was entering a spaceship. It's quite funny how that imagination of a much younger me soon would get adapted into one small section of the book.

So that was mainly focussed on a water-like world - then it shifted as we travelled further which made me think of this world where you couldn't safely walk on the planet's surface unless you had these fireproof shoes.

More ideas soon came during the trip, a few of which I wrote down and were going to be a part of the book but didn't cut it: either the jokes didn't make any sense, or they were unnecessary plotlines that didn't suit the story. But as how the story turned out in the end, I'm really happy with it!

This is the first novel in the Librarian Saga where, not one but two main characters from two separate books come together to save their friend.

The mystery of why Floyd was being erased is an intriguing puzzle. If you have stuck around for the previous five books and loved this character, I imagine readers and fans don't want the main star to be gone, so of course two characters from the previous books must save him!

But as the mystery deepens, it gets a very clever and interesting that this isn't just about someone's disappearance.

This is more of a supernatural plot. This isn't anything Floyd and his friends have encountered before, and it might lead them to dangerous territory.

It is also a great novel for previous fans as they'll get a lot of reminders here. But even if you haven't caught up with the other books, you'll still have something fun to look forward to.

It was great having Ryan and Charlotte together as I was planning on having them returning to the series but mostly coming together. It's nice to see brave and self-assured Charlotte head butting with unsure and awkward Ryan. They have of course changed a bit since we have last saw them in *The Lost Humans* and *System of Trees*, but their spirts aren't gone.

There's a lot of alien worlds and different technology playing out in this novel. As you go from one place to another, it keeps getting exciting in every chapter.

There isn't much I want to give away as I want to leave all the wonder and clues up to you, reader. Will Floyd get out of this alive? Or will he drag Ryan and Charlotte along to his downfall?

Liam Adams, Summer 2025

1. What are we forgetting?

In one moment, something shivered across the cosmos. Through time everyone started to feel a sudden change. It was as if something was on the tip of their thoughts, but they couldn't remember what it was.

But worse. A question loomed over their brains: what are we forgetting?

It shouldn't be so difficult, or they would have spotted it. But as they tried hard to recall it, their minds just simply continued on with their current activities, as if this forgetting was just a small thing.

This effect continued to spread until it touched every part of reality. Which led to Earth in the year 2011, where young bright Charlotte planned to make a difference in the world; well, almost.

Being fired after spilling coffee and embarrassing a conference meeting for her boss, she thought she had lost hope. She had lost one job after another, from foolishness or some big mistake, both of which she regretted.

That thought deepened inside Charlotte, as she wondered where she could go now, until a friend of hers called her up and told her that there was a job opening for photography in the big city.

Charlotte had never been cut out for moving to the city from her town, but the opportunity was too big for her to waste. She jumped on board the closest train that would take her there and hopefully get the job.

She been a photographer for about five months. She took photos around the city, and they would be in the number one newspapers. Photos that Charlotte took added to magazines.

Now she was given a special request to take some photography at a fashion gala where everyone wore special dresses and suits. It was an outdoor environment over a balcony where waiters were serving drinks and food. Ballons were hung above a number of big doors which led to the indoor chamber.

Charlotte didn't wear anything so majestic, other than a coat. Her hair was tied with curls, and she wore basic glasses only to be smart for the occasion. She was taking enough shots of the event but felt that she was the odd one out because of why she was there.

A charming man in a blue suit who was holding a glass noticed her, and he thought he would ask her,

"Did you like the show?"

Charlotte shortly took notice of the man as she sorted herself out.

"Oh, uh, yes!" she said, as she was losing focus. "I'm not really the fashion sort of girl, you know," she chuckled and smiled politely.

"Huh," the man said as his face drifted away in thought. "Well, it's quite a high-quality event. Most people across the world come to see the best of what we have in store."

"Well, it sure was…fascinating?" Charlotte could only say, as there wasn't much she could comment on.

"Yeah, quite so," the man added. "It wasn't our best, to safely say the least."

"I mean, the hats, why did that make that peculiar one so small?" Charlotte pointed out. "You couldn't tell if you were using a flat plate on your head or not."

"That one had poor taste." the man shrugged his head. Then he paid much closer attention to Charlotte's gear, with the camera and how she was dressed. "You're writing a story?"

Charlotte turned her head as she missed that last comment, "Hmm?"

"You're a journalist," the man said, as he got a taste in his throat, "it explains why you're so…detached by all of this."

Charlotte felt guilty about her attitude as she didn't mean to make the gentleman displeased with her. "No, I'm a photographer. I'm only taking photos for the papers."

"And what will the papers say about this latest edition? Are they still reporting that monkeys may have more intelligence than humans?"

"Well, scientists are still analysing that fact," Charlotte replied, "but we're not really that bad, honestly." The man gave Charlotte a frown. "Okay, maybe some of the stories are rubbish but we're making a difference to the industry."

"Look," the man said as he raised his hand. "I think that what mankind needs is a makeover. If that means pressing the reset button, that will do the trick."

The man walked away as Charlotte stood by herself. "Nice talking to you," she said alone, as she thought she had better take her leave.

Later that evening, after leaving the gala, Charlotte caught a cab back to her apartment to clean herself up. As she washed her make up, something struck her, something that she couldn't make out. She knew she was remembering something, but what exactly?

It was right there, as if she caught it at first glance, but…it slipped away, or something. She didn't know. She didn't even know if it was important for work or not.

But whatever it was, she didn't need think about it right now. Tomorrow she had to see her friend Samantha who planned to have an afternoon catch up. And that was something she was not going to forget about!

Charlotte caught up with Samantha at a café where they ordered coffee and some light food. Samantha had dark skin, and she had her long hair tied back and wore a similar outfit to Charlotte: casual.

Samantha was one of many of Charlotte's friends who moved to the city to get better careers. Charlotte shared with Samantha all about her recent experience in the city and her workplace. Samantha could understand Charlotte clearly as she told her all the strengths and struggles she had been going through.

"That's rough!" Samantha replied, engaged in Charlotte's recent developments. "How did you get yourself through all of that?"

"Don't ask," Charlotte warned. "It's only for a couple of bucks for a couple of hours."

"But I mean, you've been up on your feet since I told you about the job."

Charlotte had been doing overtime, as she needed to earn trust from the workplace. To do that is to do overtime. "Anyway, I don't mind the job, really," she said. "At least it gives me the chance to use my photo skills that I never dreamed of doing."

Samantha gave Charlotte a stare as she nodded, "Right," then she thought to change the subject. "Any hoo, you're going to Michel's party on Saturday?"

Charlotte gave a shocked expression. "Wait, Michel's coming?!"

"You didn't know?!" Samantha said as she gave the same look to Charlotte; then they burst out laughing. "Charly! You are way too busy!"

"I know, that's something that I have got to work on," Charlotte noticed.

"Well, just remember, you can ask me if you are unsure of anything."

Charlotte smiled. Then, as Charlotte was about to continue drinking, a ringing sound came to her head as she noticed something was bugging her that she couldn't shake off. She turned to look at Samantha, but she paused as her lips were frozen in motion.

But that wasn't the weirdest thing. Everything around her, the people, the cars and cabs, even a bird, were all frozen, as if time had stopped.

Charlotte looked around while nerves grew into her chest and her pulse raced as she breathed heavily. What was this? She thought she had never witnessed anything so bizarre in her life.

Then, a voice whispered out of nowhere. It called, *"Charlotte"*.

The voice was unknown, and Charlotte couldn't tell where it was coming from. It made her even more confused. *"We need to meet. Head over to the old railway construct at 5:59:99:99,6. We will explain everything then, but you must trust us."*

Then, the voice faded away and time resumed. "So, Michel told me what he was planning…", Samantha explained.

"Sorry, Samantha," Charlotte interrupted, as she got up from her chair. Hearing the call gave her the hippygipees. "I'm not feeling so well."

"Is anything wrong?" Samantha wondered, as she noticed something was up with Charlotte.

"Something came up. Just thought of it now," Charlotte lied, only to make an excuse. "I'll see you on Saturday."

"Yeah, sure," Samantha agreed, as Charlotte took off and headed directly to where the voice told her to go.

Charlotte arrived at the area in time, with only thirty seconds to spare. She saw the sun setting perfectly though this was no occasion for sunsets. The railway was blocked with bunch of empty warehouses and two separate railways leading in either direction: one lead towards a far distant tunnel. There were also some rusty and deserted trains that looked worse for wear.

A worried thought occurred to Charlotte: What if anyone spotted her sneaking in as it was a restricted area? She checked her watch to check she didn't miss the timing correctly.

The remaining seconds passed. It struck the time 5:59:99:99,6, just as the sun turned lime green, and the sky went dark blue, as time froze once again.

But before Charlotte could question what was happening, the sun changed colour as a flash of light appeared out of it, which caused Charlotte to cover her eyes from the brightness.

As she was safe to see clearly, she saw an elderly woman who wore a lime green uniform that looked quite unnatural.

The old woman became clearer. She was about in her sixties and her face was ragged. She acted casual as she approached Charlotte.

"Hello, Charlotte", she said calmy, "I am Queena, former leader of OROUS."

Charlotte said nothing but looked blank as she stared at her. It was like she was speaking to a ghost from the past.

"Am I supposed to know who you are?" Charlotte asked.

"We are an empire agency who are outside of your universe," the woman said, like it was a big thing. "What we do is to patrol and check if anything major threatens our reality or anyone's reality, so we can protect it before anything happens."

Charlotte made a gloop in her throat as she couldn't tell how to reply to that. "So…you're saying you're like the universe police thingy, right?"

"Something like that." Queena gave in, as she knew it was more complex than that. "Let's just say that we're trying to keep things straight forward in the history books as they should be. We're only dealing with things that shouldn't even be here in the first place."

After hearing that brief detail, it became clearer to Charlotte who these people were. "So, what is that to do with me?"

Queena gave Charlotte a straightforward look like she was studying her really carefully. "Can you explain your relationship with Floyd to me?"

Charlotte was about to say words out her mouth suddenly, until something stopped her. She couldn't explain it, but the closest thing she could describe was …she couldn't quite remember him.

She knew him from flashes of memories, but most of them were gone. Like they were pulled as if they weren't there. "I…I don't know," was all she could say, quite shocked, "I don't know."

"That's okay," Queena told her as she knew how Charlotte was feeling. "We know what is going on."

"But I know him." Charlotte said as she knew him well. She can't have forgotten him, since they travelled through the planet called the Bark, and all the amazing experiences they had together: how could they all be removed?

"I knew him. How am I starting to forget about him?" It wasn't something that Charlotte could make out. It was freaking and weirding her out more than what was happening in the last few moments, and she did not like it.

"It's a symptom that we've been tracing and that's why we've come to you." Queena told her and it sounded like her entire operation depended on it.

Then the same light reappeared as Queena showed her hands to Charlotte as if she should go in. "Would you mine following me?"

Charlotte couldn't tell if she wanted to, but she knew somewhere, deep inside that she had to. She knew Floyd meant so much to her, he was like a brother and a friend. She couldn't turn Floyd down. Whatever trouble he was in, she had to find him. She followed Queena as they entered.

2. Inside of OROUS

As Charlotte stepped in, her vision brightened again but it was soon blurred as she appeared in a large circular chamber where bunch of other OROUS members sat some computer terminals that were placed on small staircases.

The walls were entirely white, and all the workers wore the same identical green uniforms as Queena; most of them had tablets while they walked around. Charlotte and Queena were at the bottom and Queena led Charlotte up the small steps to approach a large door.

Through the door was another chamber where a row of people were still working at their computers; and there was a massive window where Charlotte could see a purple sky that was foggy and was hard to look at.

In the centre of the room was a large table that fit fourteen percent of the room, and it appeared to be connected to the floor.

"Welcome to OROUS!" Queena told Charlotte, making her feel right at home. While getting used to everything that was happening around her, Charlotte felt a sense of safeness in this place like these people were here to help.

"Our officers here are experts in tracking unusual activity," Queena explained further.

"Like what, exactly?" Charlotte asked with a bit of curiosity, although she tried to not be so.

A look of reconnection flickered through Queena's eyes as she seemed open to reveal some fact. "Whenever you feel the presence of Da-Ja-Vu, it isn't that your mind is acting up, it means that something or someone has interfered with reality and tried to reshape everything we know, like the universe is split in half. Where did the other half go? And can we still try to get them back?"

The thought puzzled Charlotte. This sounded more supernatural, as if something with great power was interfering with her memories.

"That's right," said a man who came walking up to them. He was in his thirties and hid his hands behind his back. "Causing a chaotic tear through time and space is extremely impactful for our universe."

"Charlotte, this is Duna," Queena acknowledged. "He is one of our best agents at OROUS and has been working for us for ten years."

Charlotte took notice of Duna. She thought he was quite handsome, but not charming. He acted like a casual worker who was always ready to report on any updates.

"So, you must know your stuff?" Charlotte asked him, trying to be admiring.

"Indeed," he said in a professional tone. "OROUS has been around before the time your galaxy birthed its beginning."

"Huh?" Charlotte replied, lost. "You mean, since the very beginning?"

"Our empire started more strangely than how the big bang started. Our home was founded from a destroyed dimension so we can repair and stop any casualties across not only your universe or dimension but others also. You probably won't know about the hollows, but they are quite damaging, something that no one can maintain. They are things that tear through everything in every reality and designate when everything is destroyed. That's why we are here: so that doesn't happen!"

Charlotte was lost for words as a lot of this was hard to take in. Knowing what could destroy her own existence, or just save it, was quite enough to break her mental control.

"Umm…okay, whoa," she said briefly.

"There's a lot to take in," Queena added, "It's not something that any individual gets at first glance."

"But what about Floyd?" Charlotte asked her, as she didn't want to move on, and wanted to know as much as possible about the situation. "How does he fit into all of this?"

Queena gave a narrow look but tried to hide it. It was if she knew more than what she was sharing. She glanced at Duna, then she sighed, "There isn't any better way to say this, but your friend, Floyd, is being erased from your existence."

"WHAT?!", Charlotte gasped, but she couldn't explain why. She still held a few memories of him; well, what was left anyway. How could she forget one person after going through an incredible adventure?

It only left her wondering, what trouble had he got into which caused him to be erased?

"How did he even get into this mess?" Charlotte wondered, hoping OROUS had the answers.

Queena gave a serious look as she knew she had to share some important information with Charlotte. "There's not much we are aware of as yet, but our readings say that Floyd might have stormed across some type of celestial accident, that caused him to be in this situation. But that is yet to be seen.”

“But how am I still able to remember him while I’m forgetting?’ Charlotte asked, as she wondered how that worked. Then a horrifying though occurred to her, “Has everyone else forgotten him?”

“About eighty percent have already,” Duna revealed. “You and only just a few have some glimpses of Floyd in your minds, but this effect is wonky, and we are not sure when you may finally forget about him.”

That thought even made matters even worse. To finally forget Floyd was the worst thing that Charlotte could ever do. She had to force her way to keep Floyd’s memory alive, no matter the cost.

“We’re just locating Floyd’s last location as he has been missing these last many hours.”

“Missing?” Charlotte wondered, “Like he suddenly disappeared out of the galaxy’s map?”

“Again, we are not sure what really happened during this time,” Queena explained. “We’re trying to pinpoint Floyd’s location and we’re hoping to try to stop him before what is about to happen, but we need to know where exactly we need to go.”

While Queena was chatting to Charlotte, Duna had the time to activate some sort of machine that looked like an orb shape which spun around into the bright light. What came out of it was a tall, big alien that had a tentacle face and hands, but it wore a business shirt for some strange reason.

Charlotte jumped from the alien as it caught her by surprise. She hadn’t seen aliens for some time.

"Don't be alarmed," Duna reassure Charlotte calmly, "This is John."

"Does he eat?" Charlotte asked.

"He is just John. He doesn't speak much, but we are experts in understanding, including silence!"

Charlotte had a hard time working out what she may think of him. John only gazed at her very unamused.

"Duna, can we have some other visitors here?" Queena asked him.

Then another stranger popped out from the bright light. A young human man, the same age as Charlotte, with black hair came walking down. Charlotte stared at the guy who looked clueless.

"Uh, hello?" he called out.

"Ryan! Welcome!" Queena greeted him warmly. "This nice lady is Charlotte and that's…".

"OH!!!!!" Ryan called, as he looked back at the alien right next to him. "This…this isn't what I think it is, is it?"

"I'm afraid it is," Queena confirmed dimly. "As you all are aware, your friend, Floyd, is missing. And worse than that, he had been in some involvement in something that he shouldn't."

"What?" Ryan replied, confused.

"They're saying that Floyd is being erased from existence," Charlotte explained more clearly in full detail.

"WHAT?!"

"I know. Right?"

Ryan was trying to look for words, but nothing was coming out as to how he felt in this moment. "This is terrible! We've been through so much together!"

Charlotte grew a bit jealous from that comment, but she didn't hesitate as she wanted Ryan to take in the shock.

"I know that this is alarming news," Queena expressed once again. "Now, if you both won't mind, would you care to share your memories of Floyd?"

Charlotte and Ryan were two completely different people, from two different generations, but they had one thing in common and that was Floyd. They tried to gather any memories of their friend; but yet again, nothing came to them.

They knew the memories were there, but they just seemed to disappear. With John, he just stood in silence as if he wished he didn't know who this Floyd was. He must have been grateful.

"Well?", Queena asked tensing.

"How is this possible?" Ryan wondered, "We've been friends for a while. We can't forget Floyd; he changed our lives."

"Your lives, yes. But I think he didn't think of his." Queena replied.

Was it true? Was it a truth that they had to face? Forgetting a friend? Someone who had been there, but you would never know existed?

Queena's facial expression revealed a hint of disappointment as what they were looking for wasn't there. No leads, nothing.

"Now, if you don't mind, your help is no longer required."

"No wait!" Ryan stopped Queena before she did anything. "We want to help!"

"Yeah!" Charlotte agreed; she wasn't going to back away from this either. "Floyd is our friend. Maybe more than others but we're going to be with him every step of the way."

"And we'll find out what really happened," Ryan continued. "We'll put a stop to this before it happens."

Queena did nothing but listened. Even though there might be a lot on the line, she came to terms with them and decided to give them a shot. "Even if you do this, your memories will collapse and there won't be anything left for you to remember him by."

Charlotte and Ryan gave worried glances at each other. The odds looked grim, and things got much more deadly serious than any of their previous adventures, but they were willing to take the chance. As for John, he decided to head back to Osram Star in his own time.

3. The Search for Floyd

By all they could recall from Floyd's past, he never once mentioned either Ryan or Charlotte to each other. He normally kept his friendships to himself and didn't speak much about them.

The two had a sudden awkwardness between them as if they felt they were competing to be Floyd's true best friend. The last twelve minutes passed as they waited at a bench in the big chamber where they could see everyone working from above.

Queena and Duna were doing their hardest to trace Floyd. They told Ryan and Charlotte to wait until further instructions. By the way they looked at things, OROUS seemed to have impressive technology that was quite beyond their scope.

Charlotte took a quick glance at Ryan who was looking down on the floor.

"So…Floyd never mentioned you," she said, not trying to be rude, but just wanting to get it out of the way.

Ryan looked back at Charlotte and replied, "Yeah, well, that's typical Floyd. He normally likes to keep himself busy, but he doesn't bother with anyone's lives."

"That sounds a lot like him," Charlotte thought. The way they spoke seemed like those memories were there, so how could they forget him? She didn't know how this side effect worked on them, but she knew if there were still memories left, there was still hope.

But again, the progressive fading of memories continued as Charlotte squinted her eyes to focus on something that she and Floyd did together. Just one thing.

"You're starting to forget, aren't you?" Ryan said. He looked at her as if she may be the only one who was still trying.

"And why do you think that?" Charlotte asked him, as she was having a hard time trusting him.

"Oh, well, it's just it looks like you're having a difficult time remembering."

"Well, what about you? Have you forgotten about him yet?"

"No, not yet," Ryan said more logically. "I don't know how this works."

"Me either," Charlotte said. She wasn't allowing this to happen, but then she looked at Ryan and noticed he was having a hard time too. She thought she should give him some slack. "Maybe we should start again: my names Charlotte."

"Ryan."

"I came from the 20th century. Quite early years for Floyd so it looks like a lot happened down the track."

"Yeah, well, quite a lot," said Ryan, who was from a long way in the future, trying not to reveal too much. "There's a lot for you guys to look forward to."

Charlotte paused before speaking as she asked, "Good things or bad things?"

"Both," Ryan replied, "but there's a lot to check out, I promise!"

"When I'm dead?"

Ryan didn't mean to make the scene more awkward than it was. "Well, okay, maybe there is much for you to look forward to, but you get the glimpses from Floyd."

"Right, Floyd." Then sad memories poured over them as if Floyd was gone completely. Will all their adventures go? It was too much to process, until Queena came up to them.

"We've got him," she said lightly. This caused Charlotte and Ryan to get up, with the fever of hope flying through their brains.

"Where is he?" Ryan asked.

"On Kori Five," Queena reported, "a planet that was once farmed and cropped but turned into a remarkable city full of many alien life forms."

The name Kori Five didn't sound familiar to Ryan or Charlotte, even though Ryan had a good knowledge of many star sectors in their galaxy.

"Why would he go there?" Ryan wondered.

"That's something you need to find out for yourselves," Queena added. "Your only task is to stay close with him and prevent him from whatever he is about to get into."

By the tone of what Queena was saying, it sounded like there was more to it than she was letting on.

"Are we meant to save Floyd or are we meant to do something else that you're not telling us?" Charlotte questioned her.

Queena gave Charlotte narrow eyes as she replied, "You will know in time, but remember this: if you fail in your task, we will bring you back here and return you to your normal times and you won't recall any of these events."

Charlotte and Ryan didn't like the sound of failure, so they had to pull themselves together and get this job done. Queena led them over to a bright light portal like before, and Ryan and Charlotte stepped in front of it.

"Is he really there?" Ryan asked Queena.

"He is if you can find him yourselves," Queena told them. "The interference is still there so we can't pinpoint exactly where but we know he is in the city."

"The city?" Charlotte wondered, as she had never been to an alien city before. Well, not one that was an actual city.

Queena said little about the context of their destination, so Ryan and Charlotte once again gave glances to each other, and Ryan said, "So, here we go!"

"Yeah, here we go!" Charlotte commented as they walked through the light.

As they stepped through, they could see it was nightfall, and the city appeared to be an actual city just as Queena described. There were many skyline towers and building blocks stacked up on each other. They stood on the stone ground of the street, and they noticed on the other side were rivers swirling under a number of bridges that connected to different districts of the city. Charlotte couldn't help but be reminded of Prague; she had never been there but had seen photos of it. If she had to imagine what it was like, this was it.

Then there were the aliens. All of them were different from each other and mostly bizarre. One had feathers while wearing a buffy coat, and another was forty feet tall and had spider legs as it moved from street to street.

But the worst of it was that they were caught up with a busy crowd where all the creatures were roaming across each other.

Charlotte was trying to get used to all of this weird wackiness as she hadn't done anything like this for a long time. Ryan thought he should comfort her as he commented, "Don't worry, they won't bite."

"You say," Charlotte commented back. "I never got to spend enough time with aliens in my neighbourhood."

Charlotte gazed out to see how far the city went. They went on following it and they noticed that all the bridges from across the city could been seen in other directions, like they were making a pathway to somewhere. As they went even further, five of the bridges intertwined. One led everyone to this specific city area where the river became bigger.

But it wasn't a river anymore they realised. It became an ocean and as they approached the destination, the crowd became intense, and Ryan and Charlotte struggled to move. It came to the point that Charlotte tried to call out to Ryan as Ryan did to Charlotte.

They couldn't budge as they tried to squeeze through, but they knew if they tried to sneak under them, it may be a bad idea. All the aliens were heading to that

same direction. Ryan and Charlotte had no idea why
going there was so special.

Then, Ryan was able to make a gap through the
aliens. He passed through, trying to find where Charlotte
was. He called out to her, hoping for her to respond.
Then a small voice called, and he knew it was her.

He headed directly to where she called, then he
saw her and the two met up.

"Tough crowd," Charlotte commented.

"Yeah, I haven't seen anything like this before,"
Ryan told her. "I'm only used to small spaces, if you
must know."

"Floyd must have really found somewhere which
was hard to find him in," Charlotte noticed, as it seemed
impossible to locate him.

"Well, from what I know, most alien planets do
get pretty rough like this one, so we should stay as clear
as possible if I were you," Ryan thought likewise.

"Agreed," Charlotte replied, as they made an
easy approach forward to where the bridges were
leading.

4. We Sang All Night

As they finally arrived at the other part of the city, everything looked busier. The buildings spread out as all these aliens partied.

"What's this?" Charlotte wondered what was going on. "Are they some sort of swarm?"

"No, I think they're just partying," Ryan said, as he took notice of their behaviours.

Charlotte was trying to untangle all this wackiness. "A bit weird."

"It's more than that," Ryan added, "but sometimes you get used to it."

Charlotte laughed at that comment as in all the adventures she had experienced, nothing had ever been simple.

Then they spotted a cramped building on one side of the street. It was a size of a diner and had loud music on the inside and lots of flashing lights. Most of the creatures popped in so it caught Ryan and Charlotte's attention.

"What's this?" Ryan asked, confused.

"Karaoke?" Charlotte suggested.

"Of course it is."

As they entered, the room was cramped with tables stacked. All the locals were watching two robots singing on stage. They sang a song that Charlotte recalled back home but she wasn't sure if she could accept how they sang it.

But strangely, the two robots looked familiar to Charlotte in a way; it was mostly the voices maybe. The look of the detail in their orb heads almost rang a bell too. But either way, they sang, and everyone was having the time of their life!

Ryan was a fan of the song, and he wanted to dance, but Charlotte only observed. She needed to find Floyd, but the question was, where was he?

"This is quite an energetic crowed!" Ryan said.

"Ryan, focus!" Charlotte told him. "Floyd has to be here; we just have to keep our eyes…"

She stopped as someone came on stage from the corner of the robots. A man who was dressed in a long red robe that had a face…a face…that robe!

"That's him!!!" Charlotte called out in shock.

Floyd laughed as he called out to the crowd, "Hey, how's everyone's night going? I know we've been having quite a blast tonight. Me and the bots have had the pleasure of entertaining you lot. It's what we do! Isn't that right, guys?"

The librarian Floyd looked back at his robots. LO-NO came to the speaker, "IT MEANS EVERYTHING TO US!!!"

"WE LIKE TO PARTY!!!!!" said YO-NO next to him.

Floyd was about to comment further but he soon heard his name called and repeated. Then, to his surprise, he saw two of his friends in the distance!

"Charlotte? Ryan?" he said in a shocked tone. "Together? Now this is a surprise!"

The librarian stopped there, frozen while everyone kept staring at them. He noticed that this should be a more private matter that everyone should not get involved in.

"Would you excuse us for a moment?" he said, as he and the NO bots jumped off stage. Another performer played and did their own thing which kept everyone entertained.

As Floyd made his way to his friends, Charlotte gave an unpleasant look like she wasn't in whatever game Floyd was playing, and Ryan wasn't too far behind how she was feeling.

"WELL, WHO DO WE HAVE HERE?", LO-NO said, quite cheeky.

"Please, don't embarrass me in front of my friends," Floyd told him to quiet down. Then he focused back on Ryan and Charlotte, "How is this even possible? You two don't know each other."

"It's a long story," Ryan explained the best he could.

"Floyd," Charlotte butted in, as she gave him an honest and trusting expression, "we came here to help you."

"Help me?" he said with confusion. "Help me with what exactly?"

"I SAY SHE NEEDS TO KEEP A CLOSE EYE ON HIM IN EVERY CENTURY...", LO-NO broke off. Then his head popped off and he fell on the floor, "OH POOF!"

"NOW I CAN JOIN TOO!!!" YO-NO added as his head fell off because his data guessed it was some sort of game.

"PUT YOUR STUPID HEAD BACK ON AND GET US OUT OF THIS MESS!!!" LO-NO demanded.

Floyd just stood there as he wasn't sure what to do. He picked up the NO heads and held them each in each hand. "Okay, don't you two bicker at each other, alright?" Floyd ordered them.

"Floyd," Ryan tried to get his friend's attention, "we received this destress call…"

"Don't need it," Floyd brushed off Ryan's sentence and acted confident.

"But it's really important, it's got to do with you."

Floyd froze as he thought he might as well stop whatever he was doing and hear them out.

"Me?" he asked with interest. "Does this have anything to do with my library membership card?"

"No!" Charlotte snapped. "We're here because you're in danger! More than ever before! And one that we don't know we can save you from."

Floyd gave a broken and startled look as he didn't know what Charlotte meant by that. Then he looked at Ryan and asked, "Is this true?"

"I'm afraid so," Ryan could only say.

Floyd tried to process it all, but again, it didn't mean anything to him. He had been through multiple dangers before, and he always got out of it.

"Doesn't sound like it's a big deal," he said, as he shrugged it off.

"I WOULD LISTEN TO HER IF I WERE YOU," LO-NO told him.

"Shhhh!"

"YOU ALWAYS GET INTO TROUBLE."

"REMEMBER THAT TIME HE ACCCIDENTALLY SNUCK ONBOARD THE MARIEN'S SHIP AND GOT HIMSELF CAUGHT BY THE WHOLE CREW?" YO-NO mentioned.

"YES," LO-NO agreed with his buddy - which never happened. "HE NEVER LIKED THAT SHIP."

"AND HE FLUSHED THE ENTIRE POPULATION OF SI NEX WHEN HE WAS MEANT TO BUY A NEW PHINO."

"Can you both stop?!" Floyd told them, and he started regretting bringing them along. There were reasons why he kept himself apart from them!

Elsewhere across another part of the galaxy lay the underwater world of Limnos, a wonderous aquatic place that had a massive reef and sea life in their oceans.

Somewhere down few trillion feet lay the city of the Willfer people, who had green and blue leathery skins with gills, deep dark blue eyes and feet shaped like flippers.

Their city had a glamorousness as it shined through the blue lightness of the water. Hundreds of towers peaked, while bridges spanned the gaps between each of them, and some water vessels passed through outside them.

The Willfer people were able to breathe in either the ocean or the surface. As the world was all shaped under water, the interiors were breathable for outsiders and there was no sign that water leaked in.

Elsewhere, over at the city's weather tower, lay Professor Gorily, who was an expert on the planet's climate, and whose job it was to determine if a natural disaster may occur. Limnos had records about strange events like big tornadoes, sea storms, and big heavy waves.

Inside the weather room, was a big, massive chamber that had a bunch of tables with many attachments that connected to the weather system. There was a big see-through glass dome above them. Big computers that weren't very advanced plugged into the walls to perform readings to work out whether any bad impact was to occur.

Gorily was all by himself as all his other colleagues weren't there that afternoon. He did all the studying and checking up on his maths, doing his work to calculate to see if everything was all stable.

While he was doing his busy thinking, he noticed the machine was picking up something and a sound triggered him. It was a sound that he didn't recognise before, which made him feel uncertain.

He checked what the weather system picked up. It gave him a shiver to see what exactly it detected. Gorily got up and fell from his chair, then raced through the hall and bumped into walls and the janitor.

Of what he had discovered, he had to tell Governor Ree, the people's leader. This was something that couldn't wait.

The parliament tower had a stunning look different from the rest of the city and was more recognisable. The top floor had the council room where a row of tall seats were stacked on either side of the wall. The council seats were shorter as they gazed towards the large window that looked over the city. The floor was carved in marble which showed sea creatures who were based on Limnos's mythology known as the Kreg.

No one was in the chamber at this moment, except for the governor who pondered around the room. He was wondering as if waiting for some big news to arise. Luckily, he got one.

Gorily rushed in and slipped across the floor, and slid towards the governor's feet. The governor wore a dark robe with red bracelets. He sighed as he saw the sight of the professor.

"What is it now, professor?" he asked, unimpressed.

Gorily lifted his head as he slowly rose up. "Sir! I've got some news to share!"

"Not now," the governor told him harshly, as he wished to not be disturbed. "I've got about six other meetings to sort out…"

"But I think you need to know," Gorily interrupted. "It might be very important."

Ree gazed back at him while Gorily gave a concerning look like his life depended on it, which convinced the governor to hear him.

"Speak."

"It's got to do with the Pearl," the professor explained. "It seems to be acting up. Something within it is building up some type of aura. The readings can't really make it out…"

"So, what does it have to do with me?" Ree cut to the chase, as he was growing bored with their conversation.

"What I'm saying is that the Pearl is unstable, uncontrollable. We need to check if everything is alright."

Ree couldn't tell if Gorily was being serious or what. He knew that their great Atom Pearl had been functioning for generations, and it had never had any hiccups. And he wasn't going to start believing that there was something wrong with it now.

"Then your readings are wrong," Ree corrected the professor. "If it's all right with you, professor, I think there's no issue or problem."

"But sir!" Gorily butted in without finishing his statement. "It's something I cannot ignore!"

"Then do something about it!" Ree instructed. He turned around and gave Gorily a sign that their conversation had come to an end.

"But I'm telling you…," Gorily shouted.

Ree turned around furiously and gazed at Gorily tensely. "If you come butting in just to tell me that we're all in danger, then it's not me you have to talk to. Go to your own party."

Despite how serious the situation was, Gorily knew he couldn't convince their leader. So maybe he should do what Ree instructed him to do. He could get

someone who did care about their society, and someone
who knew their stuff.

5. The Clock Tower

Floyd and his pals made their way to where Floyd was staying, which was some dull hotel. It didn't really have a top five-star reception for anyone to go to, but for some reason, Floyd and the NO bots had been there since they arrived.

It was rather mysterious to have all three out of the Library for a long period of time. Neither of the NO bots knew what Floyd was planning, but he had a purpose for being here.

Floyd walked in with both bot's heads in his hands as they were heavier than they looked. He wanted to have some time to himself before, out of the blue, his two best buddies, Charlotte and Ryan, came here with no explanation. He was keen to learn why.

So far, Charlotte and Ryan had noticed how oddly Floyd had been acting, as if they had come at a strange time in the librarian's life.

"Is it me or is Floyd acting a bit different?" Ryan asked Charlotte in private.

As much Charlotte hated to admit it, she agreed. Floyd had become more distant from them since they arrived, and he seemed like he wanted to be left alone.

"Yeah," she said, "I don't remember Floyd being so…well, out of the ordinary."

"You and me, both," Ryan commented, as he remembered the old Floyd always welcomed his friends. But something was up. "You think he's got something to hide?"

The thought had occurred to Charlotte that seemed possible. Did he know that they had come for him just to prevent what he was about to do, or what?

It only made it even more questionable about how Floyd got erased in the first place. Maybe this was leading to his downfall.

Charlotte and Ryan went somewhere to speak in private, while Floyd was sorting the Bots as their heads hovered above him. This room should be filled with wonders or fascinating things, but there was nothing! Nothing!

The room didn't have furniture or even a chair. It was blank with a wooden floor tile and only a small lazy bed on the corner, near the window.

During this time, Floyd was asking himself over and over why Ryan and Charlotte were here? It didn't make any sense, and it seemed sus. But he obviously knew something was up, like he was about to do something real stupid.

He drank an orange flavoured energy drink, pouring it in a glass while he thought about it. He had spent weeks drinking it; or heck, he been staying on this planet for way too long! He wondered again what his life had become since he left the library.

LO-NO hovered over to him at the bed side and beamed at him.

"I CAN SENSE HE IS OVER HIS HEAD AGAIN," the robot teased, as YO-NO hovered back and forward in the room.

Floyd stared in deep thought as he gazed through the street where Charlotte and Ryan walked together.

"What do you think they're here for?" he asked the bots, as he didn't know the answers yet. "It's not like I've got something to hide."

"BUT YOU DO HAVE SOMETHING TO HIDE, DON'T YOU?" LO-NO asked as he got closer to Floyd's head.

"No, I don't think so," Floyd said clearly, not sure what it was. "I'm more questioning how they got here? There's no way either of those two could arrive, skipping one timeline to another, and how did they find me?"

It left Floyd on edge and he didn't like it. He didn't like being played, even at his own toys and games. Someone must have had the exact same technology as his which must have made this possible. But he knew that technology didn't exist until the whole universe was collapsing.

"WHO KNOWS, BUT I THINK THEY GOT YOU WHERE THEY WANT YOU."

Floyd couldn't help it but LO-NO's chattering was becoming unhelpful, even in these most strange times. "But, if it's that important, am I really in danger?"

The very thought troubled Floyd as maybe he had gone too far and maybe no one could save him. He never thought of his luck running out until tonight. With all the near-death experiences he had had, all the escapes in the nick of time, could this be it?

"OOOOOOOOH! FLOYD'S IN TROUBLE!"

"But what if I am?" he asked wondering. "What if I came to a fate where I may not come back?"

The bots said nothing while Floyd kept thinking about it. The real reason why he had travelled all the way to Kori Five was that he had been waiting for a single something that he had been waiting for for some time.

Then, he noticed something. His eye caught onto something, something remarkable that he had to see. He rushed towards the window and took out the glass as he pin-pointed what he was seeing, which showed him a clock tower.

It was only two blocks away and he noticed that this wasn't any normal tower, it was put there for a purpose. He knew it was here for something, and he knew what for.

"You see that?" he said to the bots who were clashing into each other.

"NO?" LO-NO replied.

"That clock tower, I believe I've seen it before, on a paper on something, before I got here."

"SO?"

"So, it means something very important is in there waiting for me."

Floyd rushed and ran straight to it then sneakily approached it. Luckily there was no one in the streets who noticed him. He arrived at the tower's iron gates and saw it was open. He passed through and soon found some stairs that led up.

Floyd walked up as the stairs looped around in a tight spiral. Soon he arrived in a big interior that glimmered with a shiny gold and slippery floor. He explored a bit until he found a door that felt less noticeable and through there, another staircase.

The staircase led him to the top and he arrived where he could see the city in all directions. Four pillars kept the roof intact. The floor was made of pale wood and a large bell stood in the centre that hovered few inches from Floyd's head.

He walked around like he was looking for something, something that he had to find. Luckly, he found it under a curb where there was a note inside. This was what he was waiting for! It gave all the information for what Floyd needed to do and where he must be. Everything that was assigned to him was on that paper, and it would lead him to his upcoming task.

When Floyd got back to his apartment, the NO Bots flew over to him. Floyd sat over on his bed. It was written about where he needed to be as there was an appointment that he need to attend. It was written with a not common language that the bots couldn't translate.

After learning about it, Floyd quickly planned his next step.

"WHAT'S ALL THIS ABOUT?" LO-NO asked him.

"Its', uh, a contact number!" Floyd revealed.

"A CONTACT NUMBER?" LO-NO asked. He seemed unsure, and then he sighed. "DON'T TELL ME THAT YOU ARE GOING ON ANOTHER ADVENTURE?"

"Not only just me," Floyd said happily, "Charlotte and Ryan are coming as well!"

It didn't seem right to LO-NO. After his two friends just arrived, he suspected something was going on with Floyd. Was going on another adventure a good idea?

"SERIOUSLY? JUST AS THEY ARRIVED AND THEY'VE COME HERE JUST TO PREVENT SOMETHING THAT YOUR ABOUT TO DO?"

"We don't know what it is yet," Floyd said, so sure of himself.

"THIS COULD BE IT! THIS COULD BE THE DAY WHERE FLOYD'S LUCK MIGHT FINALLY RUN OUT!"

Then a crick of the door slowly opened as something fast and small hit the heads of the NO Bots, and they fell like pin balls. They didn't get smashed, but they were deactivated.

Floyd froze in confusion as he turned and saw the intruders.

He put his hands up, "I think your boss will be very pleased."

6. A Somewhat Rescue Operation

Ryan and Charlotte sat at an outside café that stayed open late in the night. But Charlotte wasn't sure how long the day takes in different planets; she was no expert. They saw mostly aliens as they were having some food and drinks at their late dinner. The street was quieter now than when they arrived.

But during this moment, they had a deep breakthrough on Floyd and how they should prevent him from going where he means to go.

"What do you think we can do?" Charlotte asked Ryan. "If we know what is about to happen to him, maybe we can drag him away from that moment and change it."

"I wouldn't think that may be possible," Ryan answered logically. "What if it's meant to happen? Maybe this is where it needs to lead and there is little we could do about it?"

"Dude, we've been brought here by people who are trying to stop these events from occurring," Charlotte told Ryan, but Ryan did have a point. What if where they were going was where Floyd must go.

But Charlotte couldn't help thinking that OROUS might have more to this than they were telling them. It wasn't Floyd that they were so fussed about; there was something else.

"Ryan," Charlotte said carefully, "is it possible that we may be facing something that might have powers beyond our control?"

Ryan gave a blank expression. "If you mean like something with unnatural power that doesn't exist in our universe?"

Then Ryan's thoughts went back to Floyd.

"Do you think Floyd knows what this thing is? Has this got anything to do with his mission for the library?"

"I don't know," Charlotte admitted, as she didn't have all the answers. But even worse, there was something much bigger here. "But what is OROUS not telling us?"

"Maybe they know exactly what Floyd is chasing," Ryan guessed, which caught Charlotte's attention with intrigue. "Just think about it. OROUS is only keeping us because we know Floyd, but they want us to save Floyd. So hopefully, if we do that, we could stop this threat."

They noticed that this conversion had become useful to both of them. It was all leading to this mysterious thing.

"Should we ask him?" Charlotte wondered.

Ryan sat there quiet. "Floyd? Are you sure?"

"We've got to find out somehow, or we never will."

As Ryan and Charlotte walked through the street, they noticed it was quieter than usual. They could have heard Floyd's shenanigans not so far away. It was the sort of quiet where you can tell that obviously something was happening in this exact same moment.

They stopped in their tracks as they looked around.

"You're thinking what I'm thinking?" Ryan asked Charlotte.

"The oddness of the silence with no one present? Yeah," Charlotte agreed as she couldn't miss it. "Why is that? It's not like everyone just disappeared."

They didn't have an answer for this. What made things stranger was that they noticed a row of aliens who wore Mexican tuxedos on one side of the street, carrying a big heavy sack of a bag. They had the big hats, shiny shoes and everything.

They all stared at each other with a shocked look as if they weren't sure what to do. Charlotte and Ryan thought best just to walk away and head back to the apartment. The tuxedo gang continued struggling with their bag.

As they went their own ways, a voiced called out from the bag, "Help!!!!". The voiced was already familiar to Ryan and Charlotte who quickly looked back to the tuxedo gang. "Can someone give me a knife so I can cut myself out of here?!!!!!!"

Ryan and Charlotte rushed forward to the tuxedo gang who tried to pick up pace, carrying the bag while running. But while Ryan and Charlotte were chasing them, they wondered how Floyd could fit in that bag. Or the bigger question: how did he get into this mess in the first place?! Leaving Floyd for one minute would be enough to ensure he would easily get into something!

As the gang kept on running, the bag eventually fell in a thump on the stone floor. The gang faded away after they let go of the bag. The gang knew that if Floyd's friends were coming to rescue him, there would be no point for any further kidnapping.

Charlotte and Ryan didn't care to keep up with the gang; the only thing that mattered was Floyd. Floyd got out of the bag relieved that his friends were close by.

"What was that all about?!" Charlotte asked, with emotions of shock and anger.

Floyd couldn't say anything as he tried to catch some breath. "Not sure, I was thinking the same thing."

"They kidnapped for you for a reason," Ryan told him, as Floyd couldn't brush this off so easily. "Why?"

Floyd looked at them, as he knew much more than they did, but he knew the time was not right to reveal anything, not now anyway. He needed to put what he has learnt already aside, stick with his friends and maybe take them for a ride for the meantime.

"I wouldn't have a clue," Floyd lied. "The only thing that I know was they dragged me out of bed and took me."

By what Floyd was saying, Charlotte wasn't buying it. She could easily smell that Floyd knew much more than they did, and she wasn't pleased about it.

"Is that it?" Ryan asked, as he was more easily convinced.

"Yeah, pretty much," Floyd said.

He soon changed the subject and his mood quickly shifted. "I've decided to leave Kori Five and head to a space station called the Harvest Port."

"The Harvest Port?" Ryan asked, as it wasn't something he was familiar with. "What is the Harvest Port?"

"Oh, I've heard that bunch of people go there just to take a little pit stop. It's just right on the edge of the galaxy," Floyd explained. "I've got to meet someone there."

Once again, they knew this was another rabbit hole that they were going into, leading to where Floyd might be doomed.

"Who is this someone?" Ryan asked him on the spot.

"You will know very soon," Floyd promised. "So, I want us to have a good sleep till then. We all have a big day ahead of us tomorrow!"

And he wasn't wrong! They went back to the hotel before any other strange event occurred.

7. Traveling to the Harvest

Gorily didn't like the result. Their ruler would not listen to what Gorily had discovered, and he knew if he had another argument with him, he would lose his job and start packing.

But the professor knew that he couldn't avoid this. It was off the charts from anything he had seen in all his existence. He had to investigate why the Pearl was acting so…mysterious all of a sudden; he didn't trust within himself what it was doing.

Gorily needed a friend who was willing to listen what he had to say. Someone who would not ignore his discovery. So he called on someone from another world known as Meaux in the Sta System: a Gommliam.

Gommliams were bold silk-like creatures with big bubbling eyes that felt very uneasy to look at, and long thick nails that stretched from their thumps.

The Gommliam, Professor Upo, was well trained on unexplained supernatural phenomenon. He was even awarded for many breakthroughs and discoveries about some activities on his home world.

Besides that, he was also an expert on his world's climates as they had had many terrible natural disasters. Fire Tornadoes where the tornado was literally made of fire; lava rain; and, bursting out of creaks, there were very dangerous creatures that swarmed in the depths. Upo was pretty much a bro on this subject.

Gorily waited for him at one of the gates where the transportable ships were docked from travel to the stars. Upo only met Gorily through a call, but by how

Gorily told the information, it only intrigued Upo as he thought this would be a new challenge.

While making his way to the city, Upo admired the scenery, as he hadn't seen anything like it. He admired the marble of the towers, and the reef leading in where fishes swam in different directions. It only lightened his spirits to experience it.

Then when Upo finally arrived, he walked through a massively large and long tunnel where all the passengers went. After making way through a couple of feet, he managed to reach the gate where Gorily spotted him.

At first, Gorily thought Upo was a lawyer, but after learning that he wasn't one but a man of science, it only made him feel lucky.

Upo walked up and greeted him, "So, you must be Gorily, correct?" he said, very professional.

Gorily looked at him strangely as he replied, "I am!" trying not to make a fool of himself. "I brought all of my papers before we go any further…"

"There's no need," Upo stopped Gorily in his tracks as he held out a hand. Upo also was carrying a silver steel case shaped very circular. He opened the case and pulled out a blue paper in one hand. It had some text that only Upo could read. "I have brought what we need that can help with our research."

Already, Gorily liked Upo. Upo seemed to be a step ahead of Gorily and seemed to have much more knowledge than he said he had, which was a good start.

They left the gate and used an escalator that led them down to a massive hall with bridges connecting to other buildings in the city. Massive see-through glass poured light through the chamber, where they could see the larger city up close.

"I've been collating what I have gathered so far," Upo explained as they walked on foot. "From what you have told me, there's something building up in the Pearl?"

"Yes, but I can't really make it out," Gorily explained, as it only made the matter more questionable. "I fear, if we leave it as it is, we have no idea on what it might do to the city."

Upo understood Gorily's concerns as he too had little idea about what they were dealing with.

"That we'll see," Upo said very casually, "but I have to analyse it first before we can act."

"I like you're thinking, sir", Gorily said as they made their way to the exit.

Oh no…Floyd forgot to pack power supplies for his ship before leaving Kori Five. Oh well, hopefully this won't be another ship that he would lose again. He wondered how he kept losing each ship? They either got blown up, stolen or were sold for a much higher cost that shouldn't be the case.

This ship, however, was rusty and unsafe - as dodgy as it looked. Floyd heard the previous owner was some famous driver that raced across hundreds of planets and used this ship to do the trick, which might have been the last bite.

It was unlikely that LO-NO would join them as he didn't want to be a part of Floyd's wild rides. He turned down the offer and he and YO-NO returned back to the library.

The ship bounced as it moved. Ryan noticed out of the window there were straws of metal flying out of the ship, which gave him a feeling of uncertainty.

He walked up from the small corridor towards the driver seat where Floyd sat on a very comfortable chair with many props over the controls. There was a pop head there, a mirror, and a picture of him on some planet he forgot he had travelled to.

Charlotte sat next to him as she wasn't a fan of his driving. Floyd tried to keep the ride as smooth as possible.

"I told him about the risks," Charlotte said. She was no expert in flying a space vessel but knew straight away that they might die any moment.

The ship juggled around and shook the small crew.

"Nearly there!" Floyd called out. He could taste the station was close.

But Ryan and Charlotte couldn't help that Floyd kept thinking that this ship was in better shape before it went 'BOOM!'

"Floyd, do you think that this ship may explode any second?" Ryan asked nervously.

"Nah!" Floyd said, very sure. But the truth was he might be wrong as he sensed that this ship might eventually bite the dust. "This will last if I keep my focus on it."

"How long will that be?"

"Seven days," Floyd guessed.

Later, they spotted the space station. It was shaped like a probe, but as they got closer to it, it looked different. The metal was rusted, and they saw patches of heated metal with bright yellow glows, and factory noises were cranking from within.

To their best guess, this must be some sort of furnace that was burning up something at the bottom.

Then, as the ship hovered up, there was an outpost leading to where other ships docked. There was an indoor bar which looked like the sort of place where biker gangs would come to chill.

By the look of it, it wasn't gritty, but it wasn't anything nice either. It was in the middle, if you would think of it like that.

"Here we are!" Floyd finally revealed.

Charlotte gave a disgusted look like she hadn't been anywhere so disappointing in the galaxy.

"It's a dump!"

8. The Troubled Salesman

Inside the bar was crowd of many visitors from across the galaxy; a few from the deeper corners, and a few who were just average adventurers; others who were probably legends; and yet others who were more brutey. The Harvest was on the edge of the galaxy, otherwise most people wouldn't be able to find it.

The bar had been all patched with wood and rough metal. Tables were stacked in large numbers in different rooms that had the same look as the main chamber.

The Harvest's intention was to be an actual harvest of grain, which it still was, but it became a meet-up place over the decades. But the Harvest was a great place for business since it was so far out no one could intervene.

Over at a table lay six blue and green scaled reptilians with different coloured capes. They grumbled to themselves as they mourned the loss of their recent job. These were Hertens, as you call them, led by Grill. They weren't the nicest aliens, as they only focussed on their own gain and wits. They were cunning and greedy - snarly even.

They were just having their soil soups with noodles, and Grill growled as he slammed his fist on the table. "Bah! Why do fools like them always get what they want?!"

The others roared as they agreed with their leader.

"Yeah!" one commented. "Them and their city!"

"Them and their people!"

"Them and their cats!!!!"

As time went on, two of their crew got separated; one was left stranded and cut away from them, and another called it quits, as he knew they weren't achieving much.

But this was the last remaining six, the last Hertens who had escaped from their own realm and were trapped in this galaxy. They had a rough start, but they lived on, and they continued to live that way until they finally got what they deserved.

"Hmm," Grill thought to himself, as he studied hard how the Hertens had fallen so suddenly. How far had they come from being supreme lords to getting to this spot? If their great leaders could have seen them now, they would have been disgusted and exiled them.

"After all our efforts, is this how the universe repays us? A couple of loaf worms, swimming from one ditch to another, with plans falling apart wherever we go."

"Why would the universe care?" said one of the Hertens, who grumbled. "It didn't do much for us ever since we got here."

"We thought conquering the universe would be easy?" said another. "Why does it have to be crowded with so many people?"

"Don't forget, it's just us six now. Back in our home, our rulers had an army of hundreds who fought and ruled areas in our domain."

"But we're not in our realm anymore, are we?"

But as Grill thought about it, it only angered him, thinking that he had let his own kind down, dishonouring the legacy. "I say, I will not stand for this!" he roared.

"No matter what the universe may think, we will not
give up! We shall prove ourselves and conquer the
cosmos! We will make our ancestors proud!"

The Hertens cheered as they lifted up their bowls.
They knew they had won nothing but they would cherish
what they had. Nothing shall destroy them! No matter
how a small a stumble it was!

"For our great leader, Grill!!!!"

"For the many future victories of tomorrow!"

"For our kind, the Hertens!!!!"

"The Hertens!!!!" they all roared.

Floyd and his buddies made their entry and they
saw how unpleasant the place was inside. It gave a
dagger-like feel, like someone wanted to ambush you
when you least expected it. Most of those who were here
were villains and thieves, while others were cunning
heroes or outlaws. Even robots had some sneaky
appearance in the room.

As they walked in, Charlotte and Ryan kept a
distance from Floyd who made himself right at home.
They avoided some of the locals who were rough
looking. Some weren't, as they just sat there, not paying
any attention to them.

A small droid that was a flat disk and the size of someone's foot, banged into Ryan, who didn't notice it.

"AH, EXCUSE ME, YOU'RE IN MY WAY," said the droid.

Ryan looked down to it, quite startled. "Oh! Um, ah, why…"

"GET OUT OF THE WAY!!!!" it yelled.

Ryan moved and it speed through the room.

Ryan lost track of Floyd and Charlotte. They must have gone ahead of him. "Oh, dang!" he said to himself as his head turned in every direction to catch them. "Okay, okay, Ryan. Just keep looking for them and avoid any trouble," he said to himself.

As he was searching for them, he found one guy who looked pretty cool, who was revealing some compelling stories to a few other individuals who were interested. He had dark skin with robotic legs, and he was telling the latest instalment of the Legendary Daryl Ra Fow!

"Have you ever heard of a space bear?" he asked the crowd.

"No!" said one of the strangers who was keen to hear what may happen next.

"Really?" Daryl said in shock. "I've come across one at one of the nearest moons of Micros. There it hit the moon surface when it saw me! The bear flew straight in my direction! I only had a matter of seconds to move before its claws would get me!"

"What happened next?!"

"I dodged out of the way as it lashed its paws. Then I tried to get to my ship, but it tackled me to the moon's ground!" Then the crowd gasped, even Ryan. "I tried to move around it! Over and over, I was pinned down! Then I pushed it away as I leapt out of the way, but it still came back!"

"It what?!"

"Yes!" Daryl corrected. "I had to leap over the beast to reach my ship! I jumped high in midair, and the beast missed me, only by inches, until I flew away and escaped with no major casualty!"

Everyone cheered as they could listen to Daryl's stories forever. Even Ryan was so fascinated as he forgot what he was doing.

Floyd and Charlotte arrived at a room which was on the other side of the bar. It was a store that had all weird stuff, like freaky puffy toys, silly masks, staffs, energy drinks and gear. There were other things that Charlotte couldn't make out. They could hear and see the bar behind them, but no one bothered to go in.

A salesman with round goggles and wild white hair sat in the centre of the store. He had been very bored and was waiting for someone to come in. Then he saw Floyd who caught his attention straight away.

"My, my!" the salesman exclaimed in excitement. "Of all the customers I have had, I have never seen one with such amazing taste in fashion!"

"Why thank you!" Floyd replied back. "These are very traditional."

"I bet they are!"

It wasn't usual for the salesman to be commenting on such incredible clothing, considering he only wore a pink shirt that had a hippy vibe with some fabric and glitter.

But as Floyd wasn't really the clothing sort of guy, he moved on to more important matters. "I got a call to make. I was wondering if you would let them know that I'm here?"

A call? Charlotte thought. Why would he want a call? He didn't bother telling me! The only thing she could do was stare straight at him and lock eyes on him.

The salesman's face popped with curiosity as he kneeled over to his customer. "Will that be wise?" he asked as he didn't trust anyone's favours.

Floyd gave him the piece of paper from the tower which Charlotte couldn't see what it said. The salesman dashed off with no emotion and said nothing more.

Floyd turned around as he and Charlotte walked out of the store, which only left Charlotte with confusion.

"Okay, what was that all about?" she asked.

"You'll see soon enough," Floyd promised again. "It was a small offer that I had to make."

"To make? What is there to make?"

"It was a small job," Floyd only explained.

Charlotte looked through him as she knew there was more information than he let on.

Floyd continued, "When I handle it, we can all go home."

For the first time, this sounded like maybe this might be where it has all been leading. Could this be why Floyd was here?

"Can we?" Charlotte could only say. "What if what we're here for is a bad thing that may unleash something terrible? Can we avoid this whole station before it's too late?"

Floyd had a funny way of looking at it. He wouldn't mind telling what he knew, as it would make him at ease as the pressure on himself. But he knew he couldn't, he couldn't risk it. Not if Charlotte and Ryan's lives would be on the line.

"Sorry Charlotte, not this time."

The salesman walked much further into the station. He was passing through these scary corridors that had pipes, and the area felt extremely warm, and he started to sweat. He knew that there was some fire cooking underneath him which was why the place seemed very steamy.

But it wasn't as bad as how much trouble this poor salesman had to go into after what his customer asked of him. He stopped halfway as he buffed while he was trying to cool off. He managed to open the paper to see what it said. It gave the right information that Floyd had given him, alongside the contact's number, but there was also a sign below it. It was very faded as it said, *"Get to Safety!"*

It wasn't just a warning; it was also a threat. Floyd was not cut out to be an imposing threat to anyone, even to a salesman. But he knew that his life was at stake because this situation was so serious.

The salesman picked out his telephone from his pocket as he tried to reach out to the people Floyd was seeking to meet. But his worry never disappeared as he feared something much worse was coming.

The Hertens spattered as they had a fight with Daryl Re Fow. This debate got big and intense. Everyone was aware of the scene and most of them were taking sides.

Ryan was part of it all and he felt he must have lost his chance of slipping away. The only thing he could do was to act casual like everyone else.

"You just watch what you say around here!" Daryl told off the big leader. "I've fought bigger lizards than you!"

"Is that so?" Grill commented as a growling tone in his throat passed. "I wonder how many of those puny bones would stand against my big hands?!"

Daryl didn't bother looking at the creature's hands as he was focusing on its face. He didn't lose eye contact as he didn't give up so easily. "I won't need to. I've bumped into few folks like you. Always looking for trouble wherever you see it and waste money on some pitiful things."

Grill's throat deepened as he didn't like that comment. Everyone gave a nasty look at each other. "I would strongly advise you to choose your next words wisely," Grill warned.

"Well, it's your choice anyway of what we're going to do," Daryl said fairly.

The Hertens didn't like this guy. There was only one exception, but he was not here. It was a choice that Grill could easily make: take on this worthless meat or just let it slide.

Grill growled deeply as he finally said, "If you make a scene here ever again, I wouldn't mind finishing the job."

"It'll be a delight," Daryl agreed as everyone went back to their tables.

Floyd and Charlotte waited for the news from the salesman as it had been some time since they last heard from him. They feared that he might have forgotten them or that something bad happened inside the Harvest that caused him to be late. But Floyd knew it needed to be timed perfectly.

Charlotte couldn't help thinking this was like some grand plan that Floyd had been building up, which gave her the nerves.

"Is this what your delightful plan is?" she asked him as she hadn't talked to him for a while.

Floyd gave her a stunned look as if he had something on his mind. "If everything goes to plan, possibly, maybe."

Then out of a door came the salesman like he was catching some air.

"Message has been sent," he said, breathless.

"Splendid!" Floyd applauded him. "I think you should reward yourself! Possibly you need a refreshing drink."

"Thank you," the salesman said very honoured. "But in all honesty, I prefer to sleep in."

"You do that!"

"Ah! Thank you!"

"Just go!" Charlotte snapped. It made Floyd jump and the poor salesman headed to the nearest door, leading him out. But before he could get to his bed, he was worried about what Floyd mentioned that was about to commence.

9. New Friends, Old Friends, Bad Friends

Ryan sensed the tension around the room. He couldn't help thinking that the spat between Daryl and the Hertens from earlier wasn't finished. And worse than that, everyone was becoming rougher now. Ryan was stuck in it all as it happened randomly. He just hoped Floyd and Charlotte would be back and they would all head off.

Just then Floyd and Charlotte did enter the room. Ryan rushed towards them.

"Guys! Thank god you're here!" he said. He was relieved but knew they weren't out of the woods yet. "You missed some action here."

"I think I'm going to be a part of one," Floyd said very nervously as he spotted the Hertens, and they spotted him.

The aliens' eyes squinted like they had seen him before. Memory floated back to them, mostly because of Floyd's robe; they knew exactly who he was, and their faces roared with fury and rage.

"It's him!!!!!" one of the Hertens roared.

"We'll crush him!!!!!"

"You know them?" Charlotte asked Floyd. She felt she shouldn't be involved in whatever this was.

"No. No, I do not!" Floyd lied, as he tried to hide behind her. Not here! Why did it have to be here?! he thought desperately.

The Hertens rose up from their table and stormed towards Floyd and his friends. They arrived, bulkier and taller than the humans, like jockey football players.

Grill and all the Hertens once again growled, but not with as much emotion. Their noses buffed and their teeth and fangs showed as they were soon drawling. Eyes deepened with hatred.

"You!" Grill spoke roughly. "You destroyed everything!"

"Hey! It was a perfect plan, wasn't it?" Floyd said - and soon regretted it. The only thing he could do was to make pointless jokes that pondered his brain. He couldn't think straight.

But it only angered them more. They were at a point where they weren't interested in sitting around and eating their meals. This was the man that ruined their great masterplan of the century, which was all gone just by luck.

There was nothing more they wanted in the universe than to take on the man who destroyed their operations. He was the reason why they were in this state; it was him that caused their careers to crumble. "We were about to bring all the Hollows together so everyone across them could have a piece of this entire reality!" Grill continued.

"And you blew our chance!" another Herten commented.

"We can't go home now as our devices are gone on the other side of the Hollow, trapped, and we've been stuck here with no resources for getting back."

Charlotte and Ryan didn't know what was going on as they shared glances, but they knew it wasn't good. Floyd was terrified in his shell, and he sweated intensely.

"Ha! Wel…I…uh…see…"

"SHUT IT!!!!" Grill snaped right in front of him. Floyd and his pals jumped and backed away. "You don't have any right to make a fool of us! We've gone downhill since that accident, and we want nothing more than to end you!"

Then a tap came behind Grill as he felt someone was bothering him. He turned around and was about to ask what sort of puny being was annoying him, and he got a big punch in the face. The Herten's leader flew and hit straight on a table a few feet away.

Daryl was the one who did it. He couldn't help it as he saw this lizard was getting on someone's shoulder.

"I did say I warned you," he said, as he tightened his fists.

The Hertens snarled at this insult to their leader, and they would not tolerate either him or any other individuals having a go at them.

"Tear him apart!!!!!" one of the Hertens shouted as they charged towards Daryl.

Daryl raised his fists ready for the big fight. "So let it be!"

Everyone else got up from their tables and a few fought the Hertens, while others just fought themselves like idiots. The Hertens weren't very affected by their attacks, except Daryl's, who was incredibly strong and nothing could pin him down.

The Hertens were no cowards. Not that they were warriors, they were survivors; and they wanted vengeance! Even if that meant destroying everyone on this station.

As the brawl began, Floyd looked back at his pals and he called, "Go!!" They started to run through the nearest door.

"Why?!" Charlotte wondered.

"Because these guys are bad news! Real bad news!"

Floyd and the others strolled through corridors and felt the steam of the Harvest as if something intense was drawing them down.

"Poof!" Ryan said. "This place is sure hot, isn't it?"

Floyd wasn't in the talking mood; he was worried that the Hertens could be on their tracks as they had excellent senses. Floyd and the others came to a stop where they were blocked by a steel door. Floyd turned the wheel handle as he struggled to budge it open.

"Now, how can we get out of here?" Charlotte wondered. "Besides going back and avoiding the chaos that was building."

"Shush!" Floyd told them as he could hear something. It wasn't the Hertens, while they could hear them coming; but there was a burst from the pipes. The pipes were steaming more heavily and the corridors were fogging up as the temperature was getting even warmer.

They sweated as they couldn't cope with the conditions.

"Whoa," Charlotte said as she rubbed her face. "Why is this place like this?"

"That's not something I can explain," Floyd replied, as he wasn't focusing on what Charlotte was saying.

A chuckle crackled near them as two shadowy figures came through the fog.

"Those humans aren't used to these types of conditions, aren't they?" said one of the Hertens.

"Weak! They wouldn't last a minute in here with us," the another commented. "We're used to all sorts of weather. We're strong and resilient; the rest easily die from the unexpected."

Listening to the scary comments the Hertens made through the mist, Floyd and the others had to escape from their reach. Floyd managed to open the door and grabbed Ryan and Charlotte as he slammed and closed the door - and run!

The corridor was long, and they were soon caught with more corridors that led them to different pathways. They had to use it like a labyrinth while speed running. They couldn't look back to see if the Hertens were with them, so they weren't sure.

They found another door and noticed a bright yellow glow behind it. They didn't have time to rethink or investigate what it was so they pushed through it.

But as they entered, they noticed there was no floor or ground in front of them. Instead there was a seventy foot drop where a whole pool of bright gold lava that had metal pillars and machinery moving in and out from it and on the walls.

The gang hovered and drifted on the edge of where the floor ended, as they had to keep their balance. Ryan was moving his arms around since he was in front.

"Whoa, whoa, whoa, whoa!" Ryan called, as he nearly fell in, until Floyd tilted forward and caught Ryan's shirt. He pulled Ryan in as he closed the door.

"Not the kind of place I pictured," Ryan thought. This station was deadlier than they realized.

"Okay, we don't go back this way, remember that!" Floyd reminded them as they headed back through the corridors keeping up a running pace.

They soon weren't sure if they recalled where they had been before; the Hertens weren't anywhere in sight. Then a laser shot near at Floyd's head but missed.

"Ah!" said a voice in the distance, "almost had him!"

The Hertens were on their track and they had to gain speed. The group continued to run as the Hertens were right on their tail. The Hertens fired each laser which hit a few pipes and steam burst out wildly.

But just when things couldn't get any worse, they came to a dead end with another door, but it was a shield they couldn't get through.

"No, no, no, no, no, no, no!", Floyd moped, as he wanted to stay alive. No way out, no way to escape. There was nothing Floyd could do to get a way out of this.

As Floyd was having the biggest doubts of his life as two Hertens approached. They could hear their footsteps close behind them. Charlotte and Ryan looked around as they tried to see another way out that they were obviously missing.

Then Ryan saw something; he glanced back at everyone.

"Hey! I've found another exit!" he called.

And he was right. There was a tilted hatch that they could fit in and use through the station. They only had a couple of seconds before the Hertens came as they got in and closed the hatch.

The Hertens sniffed them out, as they knew they wouldn't be too far. They were only on the other side of the corner ready to pounce with their guns. As they did, they saw nothing, but their noses couldn't be lying. They stared in shock and one roared.

"We had them, we had them!" it said as it had a temper.

"Oh, shut your whining!" the other one argued. "Why are we always losing them every time…"

They continued to argue while Floyd and the others crawled their way upward to where the bar was, hoping that no one could spot them.

The passage led them back to the bar where the brawl was getting hectic. Everyone was fighting each other, and they were forgetting why they were fighting in the first place. Grill was still giving the big fight as a lot of people were still in his way. He didn't know what happened to his men, thinking they must have split apart on the station.

Daryl was also keeping fighting as he was like a warrior. He threw his enemies as they came, and he showed them what he was made of: bunches of punches and kicks where he used all of his might. He could take on another load if he felt like it because no one could destroy the legend!

Floyd and the others ducked their heads up over the table nearest the hatch. What they were looking at seemed like a nightmare.

"Boy," Ryan could only say, "this is not the normal I'm used to."

"You're right," Floyd agreed, "we got to get out of here before…"

Then a massive explosion came above them from the roof. Splitters of wood flew and everyone near it hit whatever object was near them. Grill was one of them as he struggled to get up from his injuries.

But as the scene became clearer, Floyd and his friends left their post to see what it really was. There, was a big floating bubble that had inside it about four Willfers from Limnos. They looked down towards the librarian who had asked the salesman to send his message to them. Finally the message kicked in eventually!

"Floyd," one Willfer said wearing fine clothing. "I am Oil…"

"You will not interfere with this fight!" Daryl told them off. "we have our own…"

A dart was shot from one of the Willfer's soldiers. It put Daryl to sleep, and he dropped to the ground, not able to budge from the effect.

Oil studied back at Floyd and his friends as he continued talking. "We received your message, as you requested."

"And it was my pleasure," Floyd bowed. It felt like this wasn't the sort of thing Floyd usually did. He wasn't royal, and he wasn't into bowing; he would do it only for a lieutenant. Whatever this was, something was obviously up.

"Um, hello?" Charlotte interrupted. "Are we missing something?"

Oil looked at her. He imagined these were Floyd's friends, so he was happy to take them on board.

"Oh, hasn't he told you?"

"No?" Ryan said, as they were given no context about anything.

"Well then, Floyd is our guest, and he is going to save our world."

10.   The Ship that Feels Like Bubbles

Charlotte and Ryan couldn't pin down what was happening; or rather, was this what would cause Floyd's demise, or did he just have a role to play? Whatever it was, the two seriously sensed that they were getting closer to the actual events that were leading to Floyd's moment. Everything may depend on whatever happened right now.

Picking up Floyd, Charlotte and Ryan, the big floating bubble hovered out of the Harvest and went straight through the cosmos moving at extreme speed. Then they finally arrived at a blue washy world that looked very aquatic.

The bubble collided with the ocean and dived in. Luckily the bubble didn't fade away; it was still in the same shape as it kept moving through the water. They headed down and the bubble led to a certain direction. The landscape of the reef was crispy with life and was truly beautiful.

Then the bubble headed down further as they encountered an underwater ship that looked like a star fish, but cooler with a bunch of materials carved on the side.

As they entered the ship, everyone noticed it wasn't the sort of ship they had been in before. It had a strong bubbling smell to it as they smelt the reef clearly. And that was not all. This whole structure seemed like someone made the sort of pools you see in an amusement park. The corridors had purple walls with dots as they curled around very strangely.

Floyd's friends couldn't think of a much weirder or nicer environment they've been in.

Charlotte commented, "You have some style!"

"Limnos's whole population is entirely based underwater," Oil explained, "but during our generation, we managed to develop cities and technology. We also were able reach to other life forms through the galaxy. In time, we keep evolving."

"Huh, neat."

"Huh?" Oil asked in confusion.

"Oh! It's a term that we humans say that it looks good."

Oil wasn't entirely interested as he snuffed and turn his head straight. "I don't get human terms, unless it comes to business."

They also noticed that this ship had all these troops on board who wore some plastic armour with large blasters in their hand. A few moved in a squad as they patrolled one section of the ship.

"So, who are these people?" Ryan whispered to Floyd from behind; he hoped Floyd had the answers.

"They are part of the Willfer's Battalions," Floyd answered, explaining that they were the army. "They are the main common species of Limnos. They have an eternal history in the water world, and they think they can protect themselves from the sea's intense weather."

"Do they?" Ryan wondered. "I mean, really? Do they have the right power?"

Floyd had a look that he might know something, and Ryan and Charlotte studied him hard.

"They do." he said. "They call it the Atom Pearl."

"The what?" Charlotte asked.

Floyd flickered his hands about as he tried to not let her speak so loudly. "It's an incredibly powerful item that the Willfers have discovered," Floyd explained. "From their ancestors, they located a mystical and unworldly artifice that can protect their whole empire. So, if something like a tornado hits their city, nothing would get scratched."

"It's sounding a bit far-fetched," Charlotte thought, dismissive.

"Actually, he is not so wrong," Ryan commented, as he might have heard stories about it. "I've studied some articles based on it."

"And not only that," Floyd went on, "this is possibly one of the most powerful items in the universe. And they're even using its power to shield their city."

Then Oil came back to them as he must have lost them at some certain point. "Ah, I thought I lost you for a moment."

They didn't continue with their convention as they knew the Willfers didn't like conventional information revealed in the open air.

"Nah! We're okay!" Charlotte commented, as she gave a fake smile.

"Good, this way!" They entered the main control room where all the Willfers were on their computers looking at radars on their scanners. There was also a wide window that curved around the whole room.

"So, this is where you want me to meet?" Floyd asked, as it was so open. "In public?"

"This is an urgent matter," Oil said straight out. He didn't want to get techy with his visitors. "We have some other scientists dealing with the same problem with the Atom Pearl. You said you might have an idea about what is going wrong with it?"

Floyd had a look that he knew stuff while not knowing a lot. But in fact, he did have a great deal of knowledge about the Atom Pearl years before he started his library journey.

"Yes! Yes!" he admitted.

"Would you care to explain?" Oil asked.

Floyd stared down into his robe's pocket as though he was thinking that there was something he wanted to spill out. Instead, he replied, "There's an infection inside its inner orb. If that gets spread any further, I'm afraid that your Pearl will no longer be stable, and your city will be defenceless."

It was something that Ryan and Charlotte didn't know would come out of his mouth. It appeared that, all this time, with all the fuss they had been through, Floyd was only doing a repair job! But yet again, could whatever was causing the Pearl to act up, could this lead to Floyd's downfall? There had to be an explanation of how it could erase Floyd forever and why OROUS wanted to deal with it so badly.

Oil glanced at the librarian as it appeared the situation was much more serious than they realised. "I cannot say what I might expect, but the government has given all your clearance to do whatever you need to do, by taking any action necessary."

"Splendid!" Floyd clapped his hands together as everyone looked at him. He said nothing as he laid his hands out. "I…I didn't mean to pull an audience."

"Do you have a plan?" Oil pressured Floyd with the importance of the question.

Floyd tried to not pinch himself if nothing went right; but he didn't guarantee that anything would work.

"Of course!"

They entered the transporting room - a dark chamber where they saw a luminating shower of waterfall dripping from the ceiling. The shower stood in the centre of the chamber as it cycled around. The dripping was happening so fast that none of them could see what was on the other side.

Floyd and the others' throats glubbed since they couldn't anticipate what would happen if they entered. Most of them took few steps back just in case, but Oil was with them, and he wanted them through without any delay.

"Who would like to go first?" he said softly, without showing empathy.

Ryan pointed at Charlotte as he wanted her to go first. Oil gave Ryan a hard pat that pushed him through right into the shower, but he didn't come out on the other side.

This frightened Floyd and Charlotte who now felt they couldn't go in at all. But Charlotte knew that they were acting silly, and she forced herself. She took a deep breath and leant forward and disappeared.

Floyd was the last one remaining. He stared up at the ceiling as he wondered what it was connected to. Even though this was a type of transportation, and he had been in quite a few, this one just triggered the thought in him that something was wrong with it.

"I'm not the shower sort," Floyd debated.

Oil wasn't in the mood as he ordered, "Move."

Then Floyd did as he was told and walked to the other side of the shower. He was dread as he got damp from the water. And then, he, Ryan and Charlotte arrived at a completely different location.

They were in a gigantic hall made of gold that looked like it was made by the gods. They knew they had arrived in the city.

Ryan and Charlotte were on the floor and rose up. Then Oil came out of the shower behind them and looked at them.

"Shall we?" he asked.

Floyd nodded and they continued walking through the large hall.

They continued through the hall as they passed through the many tunnels leading to different sectors of the city as many unique and wonderful displays were in place, with many gigantic statues.

They soon arrived at this tower where the Atom Pearl was placed. Oil led them through another long hallway where he had to navigate them through a small corridor which on the other side had an elevator.

They stopped halfway as Oil faced his visitors, "This is where I leave you," he announced.

"You're not coming?" Ryan wondered, "I mean, anything can happen."

"I have full faith in your friend." Oil said, referring to Floyd. "He seemed to have the sort of knowledge. And besides, I can imagine things will work out eventually."

Then, before the three went off, Governor Ree came walking past as he caught his eye on Oil and the three outsiders. He had no awareness that there would be people coming over to this sector of this sacred tower.

"Oil!" Ree called as he stormed his way towards them. "What are they doing here?!"

"They have come to fix the Pearl," Oil informed him. "Surely you know from Gorily that something is happing to it."

"If you must understand, Gorily is a scientist who had many mistakes from his calculations," Ree pointed out as he shared a hushed glance at the three humans. "What is this? Some alien gathering he has organised?"

"He said if he had the right minds for the job, which he has, he could try to figure out what it is the problem. He said that he needed the best of the best, so he contacted few individuals to aid him.”

It wasn't that Ree was being rude, he just didn't know what Gorily was doing. If he and these people do in fact break it, it could be important, even for him.

“Fine, but I want to speak with you in more detail.” The ruler ordered as he walked away.

Oil sighed as he looked back at Floyd and the others. “I'm sorry about that,” he expressed. “I believe you three know what to do,” he said as he chased up to Ree.

The three went up to one of the top levels of the tower. They arrived at a corridor, as long rows of heavily armoured Willfers stood on either side and led them in.

Floyd gasped as if he might have lost his heart; luckily, he didn't as he would be dead. He then turned to his friends, about to ask them a favour, “Uh, do you guys mind waiting?”

“Of course we mind!” Charlotte disagreed with him, as they were not leaving him for one second! Floyd sighed heavily as he knew there was no chance of winning, although he might regret that depending on what might happen next.

He and his friends walked in as the Willfers sang a song in an unknown language. It felt very calming as if they were approaching something beyond. As they arrived, the door slid open where Gorily and Upo waited inside.

The two turned as they saw Floyd approaching the chamber. "You're here!", Gorily called out of excitement. "I wasn't sure if I would find my luck but I'm glad that you're here!"

Upo gave an unimpressed look, almost like Oil, as he seemed he wanted to cut to the chase. Upo gave Gorily a glance which forced Gorily to ask an important matter.

"So, you think that the Pearl is infected?" Gorily asked, with concern.

"Yes!" Floyd said, as Ryan and Charlotte couldn't help hearing that something was off by his pitch. "It's something quite dire and extremely dangerous."

Gorily had a frightened expression while Upo was still emotionless. "How concerned should we be? Do we have to evacuate everyone from the city?"

"No, no. It's not something that everyone needs to get so rump about, but I seriously would advise for all of you to rush off out of the chamber while me and my associates deal with it hands on."

It wasn't something that both Gorily and Upo were convinced about, thinking they all should be a part of this solution. "Is that wise?" Upo asked Floyd.

"Trust me, by what I have learned and discovered, I don't want anything happening to any individuals. It's very important to look after one another and me and my pals know what we are doing."

Gorily and Upo shared glances as they weren't entirely too sure on what to do from here. "Well, we can gather more readings about what it is inside of the Pearl itself," Gorily suggested.

"You do that!" Floyd thought firmly as the two professors exited the chamber and closed the door.

When they were gone, Floyd stretched his arms and hands; he was ready to get started!

# 11.	The Lies

Charlotte and Ryan watched Floyd observing the Pearl. It was like five marbles that stuck together in one big orb as it stood on a plinth. Floyd walked around, kneeling as he scratched his chin and studied it carefully. A yellow light reflected down from the roof as the whole chamber glowed inside the dome.

But while they did nothing, they knew the moment was building up to this: it was only waiting for a certain action before it all kicked off.

At these moments, Ryan's and Charlotte's memories were starting to enter the final phase. Time was running out for all of them. They knew it was now that they must stop Floyd, but it was rather difficult to warn him if this was it. But they knew, it was now or never.

"I don't think this is such a good idea," Charlotte spoke up as she told her dearest friend, "Look, me and Ryan don't know what your task is, Floyd, but you should stop." Floyd did stop while he listened to what she had to say. "Me and Ryan were commissioned here to stop you - and we know that you're up to something."

"We're here, we're not going anywhere. So, whatever all this is, it's just the three of us, no one else." Ryan said having cornered Floyd. "So why are we here then?"

Floyd gave them a puzzling look then a blank expression - as blank as paper. He didn't know what to say, but he knew he had already dragged them too deep so he had to let it all out.

"Okay, okay, I will tell you," he said as he finally let out a big sigh.

He was starting to regret this, but he had no other choice. Whatever action he did would lead only to doom, as he finally explained, "I've been given a job to steal the Pearl."

Charlotte and Ryan were frozen as they didn't know what to say.

"Wait, what?" Ryan replied, very confused.

Floyd once again flicked his hands as he tried to get their voices to quiet down. "Some guy made a deal with me, to steal the Pearl and to give it to him…"

"But why did you agree to this?!" Charlotte snapped at him. She couldn't believe Floyd would do such a thing. "When does stealing something so important to a society a thing we do now?"

"Trust me, I wish I could back out of this, but I can't!" Floyd warned them. His tone shifted and they hadn't heard Floyd sounding so…scared before. "This…this is one guy you should never meet."

"Why?" Ryan asked.

Floyd couldn't say why, as maybe their friendship might get destroyed if he said one more word. He could only say, "You just don't want to know."

"The reason why I was on Kori Five was that I waited for his orders," Floyd explained. "I was finally given a sign, and he left me a paper, regarding who I need to contact and lie that I was meant to be helping them."

"So, this was all a set up?" Ryan thought as he should've known that this was way too spurious.

"Yes, but you don't understand," Floyd warned. "What he is planning is a game changer, for all of us."

"Then let us help you." Charlotte stepped in as she wasn't going to let Floyd down. "We've been through this; whatever waits for us, we can handle it."

"I can't let you," Floyd said, as he didn't want his friends to be dragged into this. "Trust me on this, this is only for your own good."

Then, they stood in silence as now they had no idea what they should do.

"So, should we steal it?" Charlotte asked if that was what they were going to do.

"What?!" Ryan responded. "Are we seriously going to fall into the same trap?!"

"But what else can we do? You know the outcome, and you heard Floyd's plea. By how he has been acting, it appears that he had no choice about doing this."

Ryan couldn't get himself into this view. He and Charlotte were strictly here to stop Floyd, but what Floyd was explaining, whoever he made this deal with might really be their problem.

So, it only left them to do the stupid. Ryan sighed as he said, "You know what this means if we do it?"

"Yes, we do," Charlotte agreed.

"And who knows what sort of punishment we'll get involved in."

"That I don't want to think of right now."

Floyd wished very much that he didn't have to do this, that he wasn't alone in this. He sighed again like he had never sighed like this for a long time. "Thank you, the both of you," he said as his whole life depended on it.

The memories of Floyd would be gone soon. Ryan and Charlotte knew what they came here for in the first place. It may not help much or change anything, but they were willing to help their friend, even if this might be for the very last time. So, they were willing to do it all together.

Floyd's pals helped him safely remove the Pearl out of its spot as they also tried to not alert any of the sensors. They got it out and Ryan hid it under a sheet of towelling as they passed through the corridor with all the guards still there. None of them suspected anything.

They left the area and moved to a big hallway, where they discussed more about their escape.

"From what I have known about this place," Floyd informed them with knowledge, "there should be a hanger where their bubble pods are kept."

"Cool," Ryan added. "How do we get to one of them?"

"I don't have a lot of clearance to many of their restricted areas," Floyd pointed out as this was a problem. "Which means we got to find some way to get there."

It was rather difficult doing that. Floyd guessed if they could go somewhere that was full security only, maybe Floyd could get him and his pals to the hanger.

Gorily and Upo sat near to the weather controls as they watched what the radars were picking up. They listened in on every single message that it was giving them. They had streams of the read out and they tried to use other tools to see if it was true.

"Hmm," Upo said while he read the paper printouts. "I can see what you have being making all the fuss about."

"You do?" Gorily said, as he knew something wasn't right, which was bad, obviously.

Upo tried to express the matter more in his words without trying to be over dramatic. "You're right. Something is building up inside of the Pearl. But there's something more to that."

"What you mean by that?" Gorily said, as this was a new detail he was hearing right now.

Upo wasn't the sort of guy who would express his opinion on anything. But he did know for sure this was major and couldn't be ignored. "What I'm saying is, something big is coming. Much sooner than we expected."

Floyd and his gang approached the security blockade under the Battalion control. It glimmered with shiny walls and a rounded counter which was not covered by the whole chamber.

They skipped the counter as they tried to avoid any contact from anyone. They knew that this was one of the many places which they were forbidden to enter.

"We've got to go in and out," Floyd told his pals. "We can't windle in for any longer than a few minutes. Someone might spot us, and that could draw in some dire consequences."

"Ones that we don't want to be a part of." Charlotte thought likewise.

"What about the Pearl?" Ryan thought as he still had it under the towel, very suspiciously.

"Then stay clear," Floyd ordered.

"No, I mean, what if people go to check on it and its not there?"

That was actually a good point. It was only at this point that Floyd had to plan finding a way out, but he didn't think about anyone going and checking on the Pearl, especially Gorily and Upo.

"Ten minutes tops!" Floyd promised as they had to move fast. "And go somewhere where we can locate you."

Ryan did as he drifted ways from Floyd and Charlotte. "You think Ryan will be okay?"

"I'm not sure." Floyd said, very unsure of himself. "Sorry. This was what I was warning you lot about."

"It's okay. At least you don't have to do all of this alone." Charlotte said, trying to get Floyd to feel relaxed.

Floyd and Charlotte used another elevator as they went up and arrived at a gigantic chamber with many Willfers sitting at the computers, wearing head gear. There was countless bubbling noises as their fingers tapped on the keypads.

The two were in total shock about how massive the place was: this was no easy mission. They tried to blend in without being given away.

"Did you expect this?" Charlotte whispered to Floyd.

"No, not really." Floyd said as he tried to look for a spare computer. It was completely full and he couldn't find a spare one lying about. "We just have to find somewhere that might keep all of the Battalion's secrecy."

It was rather difficult as they had no idea what division any of these people were from.

Floyd and Charlotte had to keep their eye out as they tried to find any hints. Then Charlotte spotted a Battalion handing over a folder to another Willfer.

Charlotte elbowed Floyd to get his attention and he soon spotted the interaction.

"You see that?" Charlotte told him.

"Yes, I do. But we've got to lay low and keep quiet," he said.

As they approached, they had to hunch over and snake their way past all the other workers as thin walls blocked their view.

As they leant their heads over, the Battalion was gone. The Willfer was busy typing and he had no awareness of the two observers above him.

Floyd and Charlotte ducked their heads down as they tried not to get their cover blown.

"What should we do?" Charlotte asked Floyd, hoping that he had a cunning plan.

Floyd couldn't find a more alarming situation. The only way to get that information was to get past the worker. He might have much information regarding the Battalion on that computer.

Floyd had to think of some diversion, some way to get his attention.

Ryan waited at the entrance as he kept clear from the people working there and the people who were walking past. He felt so suspicious as he still had the towel under his arm. He couldn't help himself but guessed he couldn't stay out of trouble.

The same Battalion was making its way out, which alarmed Ryan as he tried to not do anything. He froze as the Battalion walked past him.

Ryan let out a relieved sigh as he thought he was out of the woods.

Floyd entered the worker's space as he cramped down, crawling out of sight so that the worker could not see him.

Floyd grabbed hold on a trolley that had bunch of the folders from the worker. Either they were done or weren't, it didn't matter, as this was part of Floyd's masterplan.

He pushed over the trolley as it skittered a few feet away. It clashed and banged into the nearest wall as people moaned and papers scattered.

The worker took notice of this and he raced over to clean up the mess.

Floyd hid over at the wall as the worker exited. He zoomed over to the computer and checked on the Battalion file.

"Have you got it yet?" Charlotte asked.

"GAH?!" Floyd said as she caught him by fright.

"Oh, sorry," she apologised.

Floyd continued with his work as he located the Battalion file and found all of its secrecy. It gave him all the passages and the dial code for how to teleport into the hanger.

"I think I've got it," Floyd pointed out as he was still unsure. "It may take us a little bit to get there, but I think I have it."

"Good." Charlotte said, thinking that might be the best they got.

They raced out before anyone could notice their sabotage.

12. Escaping from the Battalion

"What is this?!" Gorily spluttered, as he was getting so fussed up by this new development. Upo watched as Gorily paced himself. "This is fine, right? Or is it bad?"

"It's only a matter of time." Upo could only explain. "We don't know what exactly it is, but what is inside of the Pearl is out of our understanding."

"What?!" Gorily said, quite surprised about the statement that Upo just made. "You really think I would believe that?"

"Believe it or not, you've got to tell your leader," Upo told him as this couldn't wait any longer.

"What is the matter?" Governor Ree said as he entered the room. What he had been hearing was Gorily's worried plea.

"Governor, we have some major news!" Gorily informed him. "The Pearl isn't what we thought it was."

The Governor gave a puzzled look as he waited for what Gorily had found.

"It wasn't meant to be here at all. Well, it was, but there's just something about it…"

"The professor was right," Upo said as he should have done more of the talking. "The Pearl is indeed unstable and it might cause major effects to not only our planet, but the entire wide universe."

Ree's expression widened as he did not believe Gorily's result at first; he thought Gorily was overreacting. But with an actual professional scientist telling him this, it seemed this was very important.

"Well, what should we do?" he asked as he wanted their take on it.

"I do not know," Upo said, "but if there's a way to prevent it, it needs to be done right away"

"May I come as well?" Ree acknowledged. "It is my responsibility, and I need to know that everything goes to plan."

There, the three made their way out of the weather tower, as they raced to where the Atom Pearl was guarded.

Soon after, the shower teleporter took Floyd and the others to a vast massive chamber where a bunch of the Battalion were wandering and patrolling the area. They stole behind some big old machinery and hid from other large creatures.

They couldn't see that any of the pods were available, except one where there was an entrance to one of their command ships that they had been on before.

"We just go on board one of those?" Charlotte asked Floyd, as if this was stupid option.

"It may be our only chance," Ryan cut in.

Charlotte wasn't in the mood to have a debate. They dodged more of the soldiers and snuck into the open entrance of the ship.

Governor Ree and the two professors arrived at the tower as they kept a normal speed without running. The two professors told Ree that the Pearl was being handled by a man who had great knowledge who told them to keep clear for the mean time.

Ree might have known who this was as he saw him, alongside his associates, when they were with Oil not so long ago.

Then they made their way to the chamber and entered…and that perfect man, Floyd, alongside his helpers, were gone.

"Wh…where did they go?" the Governor wondered.

"He might've gone for a break?" Gorily guessed.

The governor thought about it, and then he spotted in great horror that the Pearl was also gone.

"What happened to it?!" he called out, looking all over for it.

Responding to the call, two guards entered and gazed at the missing object.

"The Pearl is missing!"

"How is this even possible?" Gorily said as he was lost for words. "We had so much security…"

But then, the Governor knew exactly what happened to it, and who to blame it on. "It was that human!" he said in rage.

The Governor studied and walked to his guards as he ordered: "They must not leave here! Locate and bring them back here with the Pearl safely in hand!"

The guards rushed out as they began their hunt for Floyd and the Pearl.

Floyd and his friends navigated their way around the corridors, and suddenly they bumped into a familiar face.

"Hello again," said Oil who wondered what purpose they had on his ship. "Is there any sort of reason why you're here?" he asked quite suspicious.

"Oh, no," Floyd replied, "we're done here."

"Done?" Oil said, quite surprised. "So soon?"

"Yeah, all done!" Floyd explained. "We'll be out of your way, so you don't need to worry about anything."

Floyd and his pals passed him as they quickly picked up the pace. But Oil still had a sudden feeling that something was not right.

Just then, the alarm flashed and someone cried out.

"STOP THEM!!!!!" said the voice of Oil. Floyd and the others looked back as a few of the troops began firing purple lasers out of their blasters, which caused them to run.

As they ran, they avoided the heavy fire coming at them. They had to slip some turns while the lasers hit the walls. They turned and passed through the walls that were weirdly designed allowing them to duck pass. They ducked behind a wall where they saw a whole fleet coming at them.

At one point, Ryan froze as he spotted a control panel next to a wall. Floyd and Charlotte were only few feet ahead of him when they came to realize that Ryan had stopped. Charlotte turned and saw him as he stared at the panel.

"Ryan!!" Charlotte screamed. "What the heck are you doing?!"

Ryan glanced at the thing and made a grin.

"Only to buy us time," he said. He wacked his fist at it and a door came sliding down next to him, which blocked all the troopers.

Oil looked at them as his men tried to budge the door open. Floyd grabbed Ryan by the arm as he recalled, "If we go through this hatch over here, the pods will be there."

They made their way to the hanger where there were rows of the bubbles where they could see the ocean clearly.

As Ryan and Charlotte entered inside one of the bubbles, they looked back, and noticed Floyd wasn't with them.

"Uh, Floyd?" Ryan called out, with a feeling of uncertainty.

"Oh, no!" Charlotte said as she realised that he had lured them out.

They soon saw Floyd in another bubble where he was already drifting out through the ocean. By the look of things, he must have snuck the Pearl inside with him when Ryan closed the door.

"I hate when he does that!" Charlotte moaned as they chased after him with their bubble.

They exited the ship as they were moving through a reef as fishes passed by as two fast moving bubbles thrusted onwards.

The vessel was rather strange and awkward and Ryan had to do his best aiding Charlotte with how to control it.

Floyd, on the other hand, had no problem and it appeared he was getting more ahead of them. But they wondered why he was trying to get away from them.

"Why is he doing this?!" Charlotte asked in wonder, still confronted by the twist.

"He is still not letting us in!" Ryan explained and he knew that if they didn't stop Floyd now, he would be done for.

"But, he told us everything!"

"Yes, but I don't think Floyd is willing to take us where he is going."

Even as it was hard to think straight at this moment, Ryan was right, Floyd was doing this just to protect them.

"Don't lose him, Ryan!" Charlotte ordered.

Two squadrons gained chased their bubbles where they fired lasers that were riggy water bubble shaped. But they were firing at Ryan and Charlotte as they were the closest.

"It had to be us," Charlotte thought, very displeased.

Then, Floyd made his move to fly up the million feet up to the surface where the ocean and space collided into each other.

Ryan and Charlotte and even the troops followed his trail as they were further behind.

Charlotte and Ryan tried their best to catch up to Floyd, but the troops were firing at them and their bubble was getting hit.

Floyd was more ahead of them, and it seemed he was able to get out of reach. He extended his speed as the bubble finally drifted out from the ocean.

"NO!!!!!" Charlotte called as she pushed the bubble she and Ryan were in to go faster.

They continued to drift much higher as things were getting dire from the impact on their vessel, and Ryan knew in that moment, they would be done for.

Finally, Ryan decided to call out, "Break off!"

"But Floyd!" Charlotte said, as she was not willing to lose him. She knew this would be their only chance.

"Just do it!"

Charlotte listened as they drove down. They kept the speed limit up as one of the troops was still chasing them and were not giving up their shots.

Ryan tried to figure out how to fire back or do anything else. He kept trying to figure out the controls.

As they ducked down through the reef, they spotted a command ship alongside with some more troops in their bubbles who were searching for them.

Charlotte and Ryan had only one action and that was to duck for cover and hopefully stay where they were, as their best chance of surviving.

They swirled away from the Battalion as they swung down and kept on moving, hoping the Battalion wouldn't know where they were.

As they soon slowed down, Charlotte and Ryan shared their concerns.

"I can't believe he did that!" Charlotte said, broken and betrayed.

Ryan noticed that she was in a state of shock. Even Ryan was too, but he had to reassure her that things would be okay.

"Hey," he said as she got her attention on him. "We'll find out a way."

"No. Don't you see? We lost him!" Charlotte said as she gave in to the failure. "Floyd's gone, we don't know where he is, and…"

She was right, their final chance to save their friend was done. And worse than that, he left them behind. The two people he would have called friends, and he left them.

Then, they noticed the command ship above them as the Battalion seem to find them.

Ryan and Charlotte knew that there was no chance of escaping.

But before anything could arise, a shiny light appeared, coming in front of Charlotte and Ryan, and they released things were about to get unravelled.

13.   The Death Bomb

Back at OROUS headquarters, Queena and her group of workers summoned a portal that did not often get used. It was a giant mirror above them. They listened to every detail of Ryan's and Charlotte's away mission and knew what they need to know.

They took notice that they had lost the librarian which gave them the answer that their mission had become a failure. Especially they noticed how close Charlotte and Ryan came to having all the answers about Floyd's disappearance.

"Bring them in," Queena told Duna. He activated something on his tablet and a force field floated down with a large bucket of water where Charlotte and Ryan lay. They hit the ground softly as the field broke and water splattered across the floor.

"Hmm," said an OROUS member who was observing. "We may need to clean up again."

"Where…why are we back?" Charlotte asked, wondering.

Queena knelt down and gave Charlotte a sad and sudden look. "You failed your mission."

Charlotte blanked out as she blinked. Then after adjusting her thoughts, her mind went wild.

"What?! How did we fail?!"

Queena stood up and walked around. "First: you sabotaged many regulations of an alien society. You helped steal the source your friend was going after, and he got away with it just to leave you. And that should've been two and three. And four: you lost your target."

"Floyd isn't a target," Ryan debated.

Queena shrugged as she continued. "The real reason on why I gave you two a chance was to try to stop him from unleashing something big and hopefully find out what Floyd is up to. But I must've been mistaken."

Charlotte couldn't help herself. She felt she was being played by her friend Floyd, and she never knew he would do such a thing. Queena was right after all, they should've stopped him when they had the chance.

"Hold on!" Ryan butted in. "When did you say something big? Is this happening right now?"

"Soon," Queena said as it sounded serious.

"Then why don't you tell us what's really going on?" Charlotte demanded as she couldn't be left helpless after what she and Ryan had been through.

Queena gave a look that there was more to it than met the eye. But she realized that time was running short and thought to tell them everything.

"Floyd was tasked by an entity known as Kiner. He has been known for creating glitches through realities and erasing his presence in his own existence. He is a pest that must be dealt with."

The way Queena said it, it sounded like this was way more than a big scary cloud that they were fighting here.

"Ooookay," Ryan said. "Then if you knew this was going on, why haven't you tried to stop him?"

"We had tried," Queena explained, as it wasn't so simple. "Kiner's powers are beyond anything that OROUS can stop, and even if we do a face to face with him, he would break loose out of our control and would destroy us. Stories are told that he has been hiding in your galaxy for millennia. Waiting for a perfect opportunity to place a special plan."

It sounded very bad. And worse, they didn't have all the answers they were looking for.

"Why Floyd?" Charlotte asked. "Why did he come to him?"

"Kiner wanted somebody who was very important in your universe," Queena said. Ryan and Charlotte did know that fact, as Floyd was the last of mankind. "He was only using Floyd as a puppet so he could do what Kiner did not have the courage to do, and it was something that could only be done by a mortal's hands."

"And the Pearl?" Ryan asked.

"He left Floyd clues and breadcrumbs for only your friend to chase after. The Pearl itself is not from your universe. But what it is and what Kinder has planned for it, I'm not so sure."

Queena gave a grim look as she theorised something, "But if I could imagine what it can do, it could give Kinder anything, it could change everything we knew about our own existence and destroy it all at the same time."

Again, the news worsened.

"Isn't it like a protective device or something?" Ryan wondered.

"I believe your friend had left out some crucial information. He did say it was discovered, but it wasn't given to their universe." Queena explained.

"Why did Floyd sign up for this?" Charlotte asked.

"Because his soul depended on it. If he didn't do it, you would guess what the outcome would be."

So, he did back out, only for him to be erased. But did that mean their universe was still at stake? But that didn't solve the case, and they needed to get to Floyd right now.

"Take us to him," Charlotte demanded of Queena.

"I don't think we can do that," Queena replied as she wasn't able to do so.

"Take us to Floyd," Charlotte ordered again. She wasn't going to say it one more time.

The three look at each other as this wasn't anything they were going to back down on. But again, the price was so high, and the damage may not be reversible.

But it was Queena's decision after all. She owned OROUS and was the one who made the final call. She let down her guard as she sighed and tilted her head, "He is on the world Mobous."

A portal appeared where they could see the world more clearly. It looked like hell as the ground was rough and brown and dead, and piles of dead trees lined and backed out apart. The sky was red, and Ryan and Charlotte could see a mountain a few miles away.

Queena gave them a deep serious look as she replied. "This is where your friend is. I instruct you to wear these fireproof shoes as the planet is way too dangerous for any life to survive."

"Is this where Kiner lives?" Ryan asked.

"No, this is Kiner's endgame."

Floyd walked through the dead trees as he made his way to a big open field where the trees parted from each other. He was only few miles from the mountain as dim grasses shivered in terror for what was to come, with a breezing wind that flew right in Floyd's face.

Floyd turned around and he saw some red spirals swarming around some figure that slowly disappeared.

"Why, hello Floyd," the figure said, his voice dry and deep.

The figure showed his true appearance as he wore a cloak that looked like he was the most hidden man in the universe. His face was crispy and very ancient, but he wasn't old. He looked like he had a face of an immortal.

Floyd studied the man and asked, "Are you dead?"

"Do you want me to throw you through a window?" Kiner said as he was trying to be both funny and terminating.

Floyd took another close look at him as he thought to choose his next words much more carefully.

Charlotte and Ryan stepped through the portal, and they arrived in a very strange temperature. They knew that it felt weird, but it wasn't so heated as it appeared.

"Who would live here?" Charlotte asked herself as she didn't guess any life form would survive.

"Maybe this guy does," Ryan thought, as it seemed possible; this Kiner seemed to be no ordinary figure. He thought they were approaching a supernatural being.

They gazed over the mountains ahead as Charlotte felt that something was going down right at this moment. It might have involved Floyd and his big pile of mass destruction on the way.

"Come on", Charlotte encouraged Ryan, as she began to make her way. "If we don't get to Floyd soon, our universe may face extinction."

Kiner was much calmer and relaxed as he waved his head to place it at a perfect height.

"So why don't you give me the Pearl, and we can have this done with," Kiner said. He sounded very confident as if he would share any agreements on anything and wouldn't betray anyone, if that was ever true.

Floyd took out the Pearl as he took a few small steps, "Or...", Floyd started proposing.

"Don't," Kiner warned him. "Swimming your way isn't going to save you this time." It wasn't a comment or a threat; he was seriously going to do something horrible to Floyd if he did back out.

Floyd never walked out of his way when in trouble, even if it was super impossible to escape death.

"I might say - why don't we have some sort of bargaining agreement or something else without getting civilisation destroyed and causing major mumbo-jumbo."

"This isn't about civilisation," Kiner said sharply. "This is much more than you can possibly understand."

Floyd stood wary and very unsure if this was how he could get a good deal.

"But this is a bit precarious, isn't it?" he said quite unsure. "I think, if you do this, it might cause our reality to have quite a headache. I mean, undoing trillions of lives and an infinity of its work is too much to pay, don't you think?"

Kiner looked on in boredom as he wished he could not see Floyd in his sight anymore. "That's enough now Floyd. Now, my universe is waiting beyond my grasp."

Floyd gave Kiner the Pearl. A flicker of shiny clouds burst out as a massive bright light lit up the whole landscape before it vanished. The entire environment and its population lit up, including Ryan and Charlotte as they were storming toward Floyd.

"What's happening?!" Charlotte called as she could see her appearance disappearing.

"We're too late!" Ryan noticed. The entire universe was vanishing and was reshaping into something completely different. The galaxy they once knew would forever be changed!

14.   A New World

Everything changed for one moment. No one noticed for a second or even saw that they had been erased. It all became blank for a while, until something else took its place.

Floyd passed through memories of his past, experiencing all the different types of adventures he had been through, most of them pleasant, others not. He soon recalled his early life before taking on the library.

Then finally. He woke up and something hit him right away; this wasn't his world, and this wasn't what it looked like before he passed out. He was in a stone wall corridor where small stairs led up at the end.

His head was acting up as he was trying to understand what was going on; something wasn't adjusting right.

"What is this?" He asked himself since this wasn't normal.

He swallowed in his throat as he looked up at the stairs, not knowing what awaited him.

"Okay," he said as he tried to be confident. "I don't know how I managed it, but I shouldn't be here with memories still intact."

He knew for a fact that Kiner's plan was to erase their reality, including everyone in it. It shouldn't be possible for Floyd to still be here, and he thought maybe something went wrong in the process. He took a deep breath as he walked up the stairs.

As he arrived at the top, he saw an outdoor area where pillars held the roof above him. But something caught Floyd straight away, not in horror but in shock.

He could see all around him was a gigantic battlefield! The surface was grey and rocky, and they were surrounded with tall and long hills. The sky was pitch black, and it looked like the end of the world.

There were a number of tall towers that a few armies were trying take down. Two separate armies fought as Floyd tried to understand what they were fighting about. They wore very high-tech battle armour and helmets. Floyd noticed they were strong fighters, and they weren't giving up.

In the battlefield, Floyd could spot some surprising faces and strange creatures who were part of the battle, including Daryl Ra Row who wasn't in any typical armour or uniform. He was punching all the troops with only his bare hands, and it looked like he was mightier than his stories were told.

He could see the forces were using special gear and vehicles which fired onto each other; one even managed to blow up one of the towers as it exploded.

Then, on the other side of the crossfire, Floyd spotted his two friends, Ryan and Charlotte, who were blocking incoming fire. They were accompanied by an OROUS squad team. Charlotte wore a full armour while Ryan had a shoulder pad on his right arm.

Floyd couldn't tell what he was looking at, war? Some sort of conflict that nobody really remembered? Or…reality paradox.

This could be what Floyd was seeing: some type of paradox that he allowed Kiner to meddle with, only to cause only destruction and chaos without end.

No reason why this was a large plan in the making for Kiner.

He soon turned and saw Kiner sitting at a table in the same chamber. He looked up as he gave Floyd a calming look. "Well, what do you think?" Kiner asked the librarian.

Floyd looked back at one of Kiner's towers as it caught on fire. "Um, I wouldn't say it has the nicest scenery."

Kiner admired Floyd's opinions, as Floyd had a way of seeing things that others didn't. He sensed such greatness in Floyd that only a being like Kiner can't be. That's why he spared him, even if he pretended that Floyd's existence was still endangered.

But that was his plan. To fool everyone so he could get right to this moment, and he needed Floyd for one last thing.

"So, Floyd," Kiner said, as Floyd sat down and listened to what Kiner had to say. "What do you think is missing?"

Was it a trick question? Floyd thought. He could easily fall into another trap that Kiner had for him and everyone else. "I mean, look around," Kiner offered, "anything you can think of."

Floyd had a moment to think as he couldn't tell where to start; he guessed, "First, I would say the landscape is a bit all over the place. I mean, how can everyone reach from one place to another?"

"Hmm? Hmm? Go on," Kiner replied in fascination.

"There…isn't a farm, nor is there a Governor, a mayor, or a banker."

"Banker?" Kiner asked curiously.

"Somebody has to keep an eye out for the taxes, or things could get very out of hand."

As much as Kiner was just making Floyd speak rubbish, he was really enjoying this, as this could be the start of Kiner's new empire. But he knew that it needed a new restart, and he was seeking to do just that.

"I like what you're thinking, Floyd," Kiner commented, "but what makes this place more exciting is that it is full of conflict."

"I was afraid you would say something like that," Floyd said who couldn't imagine what may come next.

The fight heated up as Charlotte, Ryan and the OROUS squad team hid behind the rough rubber wall as the enemy troops fired their canons. They planned to head to Kiner's tower as they knew he and Floyd were located there.

They learned from Queena that if they managed to approach Kiner, they would be able to stop him and hopefully restore their universe. But yet again, they learned of the risk. It was already beyond trying to avoid him now, as he had sabotaged everything, and if they don't stop him now, they would not know what he might have planned next.

"We have to get in there if we have any chance of finding Floyd!!!!" Charlotte yelled out as they avoided the intense fire.

"We may never get that chance!!!" Ryan called back. "Floyd might as well do what he had been doing with Kiner this whole time!"

"The strike is too intense!" Duna added. "We could still fight for another day!"

"There's no other day, week, month or year!" Charlotte said as they couldn't remember how long they had been fighting. They only remembered that after Kiner did his light show, everyone arrived here, wearing all this gear and weapons and the fight just randomly took place.

They had been fighting for a while, making camp, planning attacks and ambushes, but the weirdest thing was time did not exist in this realm. They learned that they've been playing Kiner's game all this time, while he lay back and watched.

"Kiner has all the control in his hands, and we've been playing around for all this time!" Charlotte told Ryan. "We've got to act before he does."

Ryan knew logically this was a terrible idea, but Charlotte was right, this battle will never end, and it would last for eternity if no one took any big action.

But still, where they were now was extreme and they couldn't push through. Massive blasts from the canons and the army's gunners fired towards them and no one could move out of their spot. The force was just too powerful.

Then finally, Duna came up with an idea. He flickers on his tablet, "We might be able to destroy that canon if one of us used one of those void pods which can blow up the charges.”

“Then let’s do it!” Charlotte said, as they couldn’t risk being pinned behind. We’re coming Floyd, she thought.

They waited for the right time as one of the OROUS troopers threw the pod and a strange explosion hit the canon turning it to ash. They began making their way through the terrain and approached Kiner’s tower, which was not so far away.

The enemy troops fired at them as the OROUS soldiers blasted them out to keep Ryan and Charlotte safe. Even Daryl joined the fight as he tossed few of Kiner’s men like bowling pins.

“YOU CAN’T DEFEAT THE BEAR!!!!” he roared.

While they paid no attention to the big battle happening around them, Kiner and Floyd stared at each other tensely, as they had much to discuss.

“Floyd,” Kiner said softly. “I haven’t been frank with you. The real reason why I’ve come to you wasn’t to steal something almighty powerful for me, that’s so pointless.”

By the tone of the immortal's voice, it sounded like he grew quite bored by that topic. "That centres on just roaming around through different realms, and universes. You do in fact grow a little bit bored with what has been made. Even though you might know where it may all be leading."

"This is a new empire of mine, which I also call a new refresher to what there was which can begin anew."

Kiner said it like it was a good thing, even as this was part of his enjoyment.

"By all the trails and clues I've been leading you on, I was only testing you, so I could lead you to this one very moment."

Floyd shivered as he didn't know what Kiner was offering, but it frightened Floyd to wonder what it was.

"Go on then," he said, trying to act brave, "tell me what is?"

Kiner looked deep as he revealed, "This," he said as he looked around the whole place, "you can have all this, this whole reality to run, if you are willing to have it."

Floyd was suddenly shocked as he wasn't sure what to think, "It's a big offer."

"I thought you would like it?"

"Nahhh, I like small offers, like a gift," Floyd explained simply as he wasn't cut out for it, even THIS!!!!!

"But this is a gift," Kiner told him as if this was what Floyd really wanted. "Come now, do you really think you want to spend the rest of your universe existing in the unknown in a library with no one to talk to, and there's likely no other life out there? I am giving you and everyone else a second chance, so something new can start again.”

Floyd really couldn’t accept this: it was wrong, wrong by the wrongest of hands. But Kiner had a point, this could save the next generation, the future of life itself. Was it too bad to have something good to change?

A contract paper appeared on the table with glowing words as clouds disappeared around them. “I want you to think real hard about it,” Kiner said carefully. “The only catch is, if you don’t take it, you won’t only destroy yourself or me, but everything else. And if you do agree to it, your universe is gone, and no one would know their previous lives.”

Floyd did not know what choice to make. He struggled since he had been pushed under a pressure that he never should be in. He had to choose, even if this meant everything he knew, loved and remembered would be gone forever.

15.   The Impossible Decision

Ryan and Charlotte finally entered at the door of the tower. Duna placed a type of small, rounded disk that switched and turned its gear.

"It's rotating the lock, so we'll be in, in no time," Duna reported.

"We had better get in fast," Charlotte said, as she wasn't going to wait when that door finally opened.

"You two go; me and the rest of OROUS shall stay here, defending the entrance."

"Thanks, Duna," Charlotte commented.

As it did open, Ryan and Charlotte stormed in and they made their way through the corridors. Luckily there was no guard patrolling. It felt like Kiner wanted them to enter.

"Wait, wait!" Ryan stopped Charlotte in her tracks. "Where are we going?!"

"Dunno!" Charlotte replied as she continued to sprint. "If we check all over the place, we might be able to find a trace of Floyd!"

Ryan gave Charlotte a concerned look as he thought that might be doubtful. "Alright."

Floyd fought with himself as he shook taking the pen from Kiner's fingers. Floyd found it hard to take the pen for himself as he was possibly doing the worst move he would ever make.

His hand came and went as it couldn't decide. Floyd knew both outcomes if he did or didn't go with it. Then he asked an important question to Kiner, "Do I have a once in a lifetime chance to make up my mind about this?"

"You can do this at any time you want," Kiner promised his word. "Months, years, millennia, there isn't any time here so that can be up to you. But it would be better if it was now."

Floyd knew that this was something that he couldn't back away from, as this moment was waiting for him to answer. But in spite of all his efforts, he just couldn't accept Kiner's terms.

"I…can't," Floyd said, broken. "Maybe if we leave it as that."

"But you can't," Kiner told him. "Our worlds will be gone, and so will you. You don't really want that, do you?"

"But why do you have to put me in this spot?!" Floyd snapped. "I can't make a decision for everyone! I can't even check my email once in a while! Why do you have to pick someone so, perfectly useless to do a big task like this?!"

Kiner wasn't pleased to hear it from Floyd, as he thought he had chosen the right person to do this. "If I have to keep reminding you, if you back out of our contract, we'll be dead, gone, history. Or in my words: none of this will never happen. There will never be a

Floyd, or planets, or a thing called a sun, because someone wanted to backdown a deal. Now, final offer."

This was it; Floyd had nothing he could go to now, he had only one option, and it was in front of him. He didn't like it, he didn't want it, but there was no one else to do it.

Then Ryan and Charlotte burst up the stairs! They watched Floyd grabbing the pen and holding onto the contract in his hands.

"Floyd!" Charlotte spoke first. "What do you think you're doing?!"

"Guys, please," Floyd told them, as he couldn't keep the pressure up. "You don't know what we're in the middle of."

"That's Kiner!" Ryan pointed. "Do you know who he is?!"

"Yeah, but you don't know what I got in my hand."

"What is it?" Charlotte asked as she examined it in her view.

"It's our reality, the fate of it."

Ryan's and Charlotte's looks were unremarkable as they thought things couldn't get worse.

"Oh", Ryan spoke lightly.

"Yeah, and if I break it, everything will be gone, permanently!" Floyd said, very crystal clear that he had to do this part alone. He was not digging in or out of anything on this one, this time he had to face it, even if this might be his end. No escape, or plan or action to save the day.

....

...

…except for one thing.

Floyd took the most stupid action that he thought was worth a try! He tore up the paper in half as Kiner and the others watched in horror as they couldn't believe what he had done. Even Kiner was lost in the moment as he didn't realise what a poor decision he had made.

But that was not the worst for him; his empire would be dismissed, gone!

Floyd closed his eyes as he was bracing for what was to come, that everything might have an ending, but not what he wanted.

Seconds pass, as suddenly, Floyd opened his eyes again, he noticed that he was still around, and same went for his friends.

"Oh, hi guys," he said normally, "you're still here?"

"We shouldn't be," Charlotte said as they checked if anything did change.

But it became clearer as Floyd picked up the torn pieces and looked back at Kiner. "This doesn't destroy all of us, it only destroys you."

Kiner was broken. He had run out of tricks, which he though was impossible. Besides being rageful or showing emotion, he only said, "Good move."

Floyd noticed that if he broke the one thing in the track of an immortal, Floyd could've easily destroyed the whole universe completely or weakened it or even destroyed the entity.

Kiner's form was dissolving while a flicker of the torn pieces flew up in the air as his face cracked and crumbled like soil dirt. He weakened as he was finally defeated. He looked at Floyd and his friends as he had only had one last thing to say to the librarian before he was done.

"We could have been a great team, you and me." Kiner said.

"Oh no", Floyd thought. "It was only you." As Kiner finally looked at him in his last moments, his form turned into a ball of light as it burst into the sky.

The towers randomly blew up and the troops weren't sure what to make of it. They looked up at the mysterious ball, except for Daryl who screamed to victory, "TO GREATNESS! TO GREATNESS!"

Then all of a sudden, a bright light blinded the whole world as everything went white and no one was sure what happened next.

In one moment, something shivered across the cosmos and time that no one ever questioned. Was it a duck swimming through a lovely lake and was going about its day, or was it just a fly banging onto a tree by mistake? No one had the answer, and they seemed to not notice.

Everyone and every world were back where they should be, as Kiner had lied about their reality not going back to normal.

During this moment, Floyd, the only person who had recalled these events, was finally free, after Kiner's defeat. By not everything was done yet.

He returned the Atom Pearl back to Limnos, as the thing that Kiner had placed inside of it was gone completely. It was just an empty shell, that still functioned in its city as it always had been.

OROUS was in relief after Floyd had put everything back as it should be, and their reality was safe. It gave most of the team some down time as there wouldn't be any major incidents on their radar in some time.

Everyone, including John, shamedly, still had their memories about their librarian. The effect of forgetting never really occurred to them or that he nearly faced extinction.

Charlotte had her morning bright and sunny, and she couldn't remember a single thing about her recent adventure. But she had other adventures ahead of her, as she and her friends decided to go to Michel's party after all.

She was about finished her job for the day and she was making her way to her apartment, when she spotted a familiar face at the entrance of the building.

"Floyd?" she said, as this was a surprise to her.

Floyd looked suspicious as if he was caught in the act as if he didn't know she was coming.

"Oh! Charlotte!" he said startled. "Its…uh, nice to see you again!"

Charlotte couldn't help but have a strange feeling. The only thing that came to her to say was, "I wasn't expecting to see you here."

"Oh!" he said as he recalled. "Well, it's a bit of a surprise to me too. I was meant to be somewhere else, but I came here. Funny how things work, eh?"

"Yeah, yeah. Still, you have to organise something soon. By the week I've been having, I need a breather."

"I've been awfully busy if you must know," he added. "Well, I'll try making it up for you. But right now, I better be off!"

"Okay." Charlotte said with a smile, "Don't be too long."

They made their goodbyes, then Charlotte soon realised something as she turned back to Floyd, "Why were you at my doorstep?"

Floyd looked at her very blankly, "You live here?"

"Yeah," Charlotte laughed, "what made you come here?"

"Oh, just dropping off a 'thank you' present for a friend", he said as he didn't give out much more than that.

As they finally departed, he smiled as it seemed funny that Floyd was the only one who remembered all the events that happened. He wondered who else did?

THE END

Appendix

Liam the Author

This Appendix is included for those who are interested in how Liam became an author and how he develops his ideas. Liam hopes that this can create understanding that people with his disabilities can have great things to say and share with the world. Liam also hopes that all those who share his disabilities and want to write can hopefully benefit from learning about how he does it.

Liam often starts with notes for a story but finds handwriting much more difficult than two-finger typing. He then brainstorms an outline of ideas for the plot.

When he writes the actual story he just doesn't stop till it's done, usually within a few weeks. When Liam started his business in August 2022, he had written the base stories of around 10 stories which he is gradually editing and printing. (Now he has added about four more).

After the base story is done, Liam takes his time to come back in to do edits of the story and try to improve his spelling and grammar as best he can. This can take quite a while. When he is happy with it, he hands on to his mum to edit for spelling and grammar that he has not been able to do.

His mum tries to keep Liam's own way with words as much as possible – hence the books are not like professionally edited books, and his mum is not perfect either! The books are the proud work of her son with disability, so she does not want to detract from the authenticity of that, while still making them readable to others. She then hands back to Liam so he can correct anything she has misunderstood. Sometimes they have discussions during editing to work out what Liam actually meant and how to best say it. When Liam is happy, his mum does a final read, correcting any outstanding errors she can find, and its ready for printing.

Before Liam could read and write, (which was not till late in his teen years), but as soon as he could hold a crayon, Liam was prolific with his storytelling using pictures. Generally, these were long comic-strip-type stories. An example of this is the final attachment. Liam has folders and folders of these picture stories.

Below is Liam's original brainstorm/outline for The Man Everyone Forgets, which contains all major plot and character ideas.

THE MAN THAT EVERYONE FORGOT

1. Charlotte have tries to have a normal day, but something's not right, also she gets a message from OROUS and meet them at 11:59.9999999,9998x321
2. Charlotte gets around OROUS and meet Ryan and John. OROUS tells them about what's going wrong with Floyd and they must find him and find out what he is about to do.
3. Ryan and Charlotte arrive at a alien city, and later find Floyd and the NO bots at a Karryokie.
4. Ryan and Charlotte try to find out what's worng with Floyd, but Floyd gets kidnap that night.
5. In the underwater city, a scintis ties to warn his govner about the upcoming treat, and Ryan, Charlotte and Floyd head out of space as they try to still seek what's Floyd is going to do.
6. The retails come back to earth after Floyd blow their plan, the scintis hire another one to help him.
7. Floyd arrived at the salesman's station.
8. Accounter with the retails and rescued by the people from the under water city as Floyd request them something he promise.

9. Floyd and the others arrive at the water ship and meet the captain.
10. They travel to the tower as Floyd plan to steal the marble.
11. The captain, Ryan, and Charlotte learn about Floyd's plan as they later get caught and stay in prison.
12. The two guards help them out as they draw their escape.
13. OROUS saves Ryan and Charlotte and they must help Floyd quickly, and Floyd meets the devil.
14. Floyd gets stuck from the prevous books.
15. The battlefront.
16. Floyd gives the marble back as they try to save the planet, and wish Charlotte and Ryan goodbye to their own time.

It's been a while since Charlotte last met Floyd, about two years in fact. with her life trying to be uncompacted as it is, she gets a message to the Group called OROUS, who need her help.

She later meets them as they bring her and Ryan together, they tell them that Floyd is missing or about to be erase from existance. Charlotte and Ryan brace an adventure once again into the cosmos.

The weird thing as she finds out is they don't quite remember who Floyd is.

This makes a more serous statroion as they have to make a journey that would help the fate of Floyd, and find him before it's too late.

Charlotte jumped out from the alien behind her with a fright.

"don't be alarmed" said the OROUS agent, "this is John".

"does he eat?" she ask.

"his just John. He doesn't speak much, but we are experts of understanding, including: silance".

A underwater city glim with light as the shiny towers glare to the ocean above them. On one of the towers at the top floor, at the coucle, there was a dome shape windows that could been seen throw the giant walls behind the coucle, there were also one at the celling as well as everyone could see the top. The coucle seats were at front of the room to face the tall seats of the addiances.

They later get ported from this large floating bubble where it leap them to a under water planet where they arrive at a star fish shape ship. The inside smell like a bubbling water and the place looked like it built by people who made pool amusement parks, lot of light of purple and lot of camler lime. Hallways curl with their walls full of dots.

Floyd gets trapped throw moments from the last few books.

After Floyd got out, he arrives to a world that the evil one created into a battlefront world, the serface grey and rocky. Floyd and the evil one were in a tower as they played chest.

Floyd also notice that Chottlate and Ryan looked different, Chottlate worn a heavy si-fi solder amora that is like its from a big burget film that had a lot of special effects. It was blueish green with purple tiles around her amora.
Ryan had a battle plat on his shoulder and was carrying two blasters.

Inside the ship, they had to go throw a shower waterfall that was dripping from the top right blow. It in a cycle with water flashing past, you don't know what your really walking into.
"I'm not the shower sort" said Floyd.
"move!" said the solder.
As they enter and exit the shower right away, they arrive in the tower.

A small drone bumps into Ryan's feet, "AH, EXCUSE ME, YOUR IN MY WAY".
"oh, my, ah, why…".
"GET OUT OF THE WAY!!" the small drone shouted, Ryan jumped as he let the drone through.

They later go to a saleman's space stasion for a stop, they meet a guy who had robotic legs (will appear in the final battle and appers in more Floyd's books) and has a tale when he face a space bear, and a salesman who had range of collectbles. And…The Retails are back!

A portion of Chapter 2 is reproduced here in Liam's words written as best as he can, before his mum edits.

2) Inside of OROUS

As Charlotte stepped in, her vision brightens and soon was blurred as she appeared in a large cycler chamber where bunch of other OROUS members sat some computer terminals that was placed on small staircases.

The walls were entirely white, and all the workers wore the same idcital green uniform like Queena, most of them had tablets while they walked around. Charlotte and Queena were centred at the bottom as Queena led Charlotte up the small steps as they approach a large door.

Through was another chamber where row of people was still working at their computers, and there was a massive window where Charlotte couldn't tell what she was looking at. There was a pink and purple texture through the fogginess, but it was really difficult to discover what it really is.

In the centre of the room was a large table that was fitting fourteen percent of the room as it appeared to be contacted to the floor.

"Welcome to OROUS", Queena told Charlotte as she was making her feel right at home. While getting use to everything that's happening around her, Charlotte felt a sense of safeness in this place like these people are here to help.

"Our officers here are experts on tracking unusual activity", Queena explained further.

"Like what, exactly?", Charlotte asked with a bit of curiosity, as she tried to not be so.

A look of reconnection flickers through Queena's eyes as she seemed opened to reveal some fact, "whenever you feel the present of Da-Ja-Fu, it isn't that your mind is acting up, it means that something or someone has interfered with reality and try to reshape everything we know, like the universe split in half. Where did the other half go? And can we still try to get them back?".

The though puzzled Charlotte as this sounds more supernatural, as if something with great power is interfering with her memories.

"That's right", said a man who came walking up to them who was in his thirties whom hid his hands behind his back, "causing a chaotic tare through time and space is an extremely high risk for our universe".

"Charlotte, this is Duna", Queena acknowledges, "he is one of our best agents and have been working for us for ten years".

Charlotte took notice of Duna as she though he was quite handsome, but not charming. He acted like a casual worker whose always ready to report on any updates.

"so, you must know your stuff?", Charlotte asked him.

Liam telling his stories through cartoons
(before he could use words well enough to write)

Liam drew pictures from an early age, setting out his stories in his comic form, often divided into chapters. He was prolific in his comic-story drawing all through his childhood. Below is one example of his cartooning.

www.ingramcontent.com/pod-product-compliance
Lightning Source LLC
Chambersburg PA
CBHW042030120726
47911CB00025B/406